I0708888

Aftermath

Heather Finnes

Copyright © 2024 by Heather Finnes

All rights reserved.

No portion of this book may be reproduced in any form without written permission from the publisher or author, except as permitted by U.S. copyright law.

Contents

The Burning Station

~ Mahila Police Thana ~

Bam! The sound echoed!Inside the station it was hell! The bagging of broken walls was worsening the fire... The things were smoldering...The flames were rising as crackers...

Outside there people running here and there... The news media officers, reporter were just depicting the situation to the camera for its audience. No one dared to enter the police station.Why will they risk their own lives & save the one's who once were a security to them.

The five patriots were still inside the burning station. People outside were just recording the incident rather calling a fire brigade to calm the fire.

"Aree koi aag bhujane wali gaadi ko bulao " A wiseman roared.

" Arre pagal bhaag yaha se apni jaan pyaari ho toh...nai toh khud karle call " Another one yelled.

Listening to the person the wiseman too left.The police officers who never thought of their lives while serving the country and its people were now left alone in the burning station.

Soon a wailing sound was heard....Hussh! A fire truck finally arrived. The reporters cleared the path and the fire fighters started their work.They started shooting water in form of carbon dioxide and many gases.

Almost one hour that fire fighters were doing their job but the fire was not at all calmed.

"Sir...lagta nhi andar koi jinda hoga...." A fire fighter told his senior.

" Hum kuch bhi karke ye aag bhujani padegi...Aise toh nai chod sakte" The senior spoke.

And they continued...________

" Dhyaan se le chalo...kisi ko bhi kuch nhi hona chahiye..." A person ordered to someone.

Yess! Someone was rescuing the MPT officers secretly.From the back door of the station.

Soon all the officers were rescued and put in a ambulance with a lighting but no siren to be safe.

Here,on another side the fire fighters were busy chasing the fire when the COMMISIONER AND DSP arrived.

As soon as the both seniors arrived the live telecast was stopped nothing was shared with the public.

" Sir hume nhi lagta ki aapke officers bach payenge...Nuclear bomb tha sir thane mein.." The head of the fire fighter declared.

The officers just looked at the station.

" Sir inke pariwaar walo ko khabar kar deni chahiye..." The DSP said.

" Kya khabar denge...Woh sehen kar payenge..? Jo mahila police thana har wakt kisi bhi tarah ke mission ke liye taiyaar hojayega...woh woh aag mein chale gye....? " Commisioner said being frustrated.

" Inme se koi common hoga...jo unke pariwaar walo mein kisi se jaanta ho unhe khabar de dijiye....aur investigation team appoint kar dijiye...har haal mein hume ye karne wala insaan chahiye...." The commisioner again ordered.

"Ji sir..." DSP agreed and both left.________

A girl in her mid twenties was standing seeing the burning station with tears in her eyes.

" Madam sir...Karishma madam...Cheetah..Pushpee...Billu ji..jaldi bahar aaiye na....hume humare thane ko bachana hai....jaldi aaiye..." Saying so she tried to barged in but was stopped by a firm hand.

" Aap yaha...? Wo dekhiye na...unhe bachaiye na koi...." The girl in her mid twenties said to the person present.

" Tum chalo yaha se.. " The person said.

" Nai...main unlogo ko aise akele nhi chod sakti....mujhe bachana hai unhe..." She again cried.

" Tum pagal ho...chalo yaha se....." The person took her

Saviour

"Aap kaha le jaraho mujhe...mujhe unhe bachana hai...." Santosh said as the other person started the car.

" Pagal ho tum...waha aag dekhi haina...Jinda nhi bach paogi..." The person said.

" Na bacchu jinda...mere zindagi ka sabse khubsurat hissa hai wo log aise kaise marne chod du unhe...." Santosh again cried.

" Mujhe chodo..." Santosh said as the person stopped the car & took her to a room.

" Tum mujhe yaha kyu laayi ho....Kahi tumne ye sab nhi kiya..aur ab mujhe marna chahti ho...? " Santosh said being suspicious.

" Mujhe laga tum sudar gayi ho...madam sir ko bhi phasa liya....kyu madat ki unki...kyunki ye sab karna tha...." Santosh shouted.

"Yaar kitni bad bad karti hai tu...shaant hoja...maine kuch nhi kiya hai...M ai advocate Shivani Pawar hu ekbar sudar gyi toh phir nhi bigdegi...कळलं ..?" The person,the saviour was non other than Shivani said.

"Toh mujhe yaha kyu laayi ho...? " Santosh asked.

"Waha uss खोली mein jaake dekhle" Shivani said pointing towards a room.

Writer's POV

As Santosh approached towards the room the view made her happy for a second but sad the next moment.The five patriots lying on a bed with ample of machines attached to their body and doctors examining them. Santosh's eyes welled up seeing her near & dear one's condition also why wouldn't the people who were always had a charming aura were now on the bed lifeless. Santosh tried to get in but failed as the doorkeeper stopped her.Shivani came and took her back in the hall.

" Ab hua vishwaas ki mein sach mein sudar gyi hu...Ab toh shaant hoja.. kabse roye jarahi hai...Mujhe kaisa toh horaha hai dekh ke..." Shivani said while her hands on Santosh's shoulders.

" Thank you....aap janti nhi hai...Kitna accha kaam kiya hai aapne..." Saying so she hugged Shivani.

" Tera pariwaar hai janti hu...par mera bhi pariwaar hai wo...kya kuch nhi kiya hai un sabne mere liye..." Shivani said remembering moments spent with MPT as well as caressing Santosh's hairs lovingly.

" Par ye sab kiya kisne...? " Santosh said breaking the hug.

" Woh toh jab ye log thik hojayenge tab hi pata lagega..." Shivani said wiping own's tears.

" Aur sorry...wo mein jyaada bol gyi aapko...kuch samaj nhi aaraha tha isiliye..." Santosh expressed her guilt.

" Aree koi वांदा nhi re...mai jaanti hu tujh pe kya bit rahi hai...Isiliye kuch nhi boli nhi toh Ye shivani khud ke baare mein bura kabhi sunke nhi leti..." Shivani said smiling.

" Chal 5 ghante travel kar aayi hai...bhook lagi hogi..mai kuch laati hu khane ke liye..." Shivani said getting up.

" Waise hum kaha hai iss wakt...lucknow toh nhi hai ye..." Santosh asked looking outside the window.

" Lucknow nhi hai ye...ye mera गाव hai...." Shivani said smiling.

" Chakorgao mein hai hum..Uttar pardesh se bohot dur....Maharashtra mein..." Shivani said.

" Yaha hum tak koi nhi pohoch payega..." Shivani said to Santosh.

" Mai khana laati hu..." Shivani went.

Writers POV

~ Chakorgao ~(Fictional)

In the lap of Maharastra there was village named ChakoragaoA village full of positive aura.Known as the moon's favourite place.Hence the villagers named it on the name of the bird Chakora.Chakora, a bird which lives its life by feeding upon the moon's beams.The village had greenery all over. Birds chirping on trees radiating positive energy leaving no place for negative energy. The people here were always happy & laughing. These people too had their problems but the energy here gave them the strength to solve the problems laughing all the way.The village also symbolized love & longing.-------

" Waise ye ghar kiska hai" Santosh asked.

" Ye mere आजी -आजोबा ka वाडा hai....6 saal hogaye unhe guzare hue....par jab bhi yaha aati hu bohot sukoon mehsoos hota hai..." Shivani said getting lost in her past.

" Sach mein bohot shaanti hai yaha..." Santosh said.

Writers POV

Situated in Chakorgao there was an ancient big house known as वाडा in the native language of Maharashtra i.e marathi.The house was moderately big giving olden good vibesAt the centre there was ground known as "आंगण " where kids or elder would spend there evenings happily.Also a tulsi vrindavan situated in centerFurther there were rooms not as posh as any 5 star hotel but more than comfortable.---

" Wo sab log thik hojayenge na...?" Santosh asked.

" Tu chinta mat kar iss gao ki hawa itni acchi ki koi yaha jyaada der bimaar nhi reh payenga..." Shivani said calming Santosh down.

" Hume ye case unofficially solve karna hoga..." Shivani said.

" Woh toh hai...par hum dono kaafi thodi honge...aur bhi koi chahiye hume..." Santosh spoke.

" Maine binni ko toh bula liya hai... Magar police department mein se koi kaise aayega...? Hume secretly mission solve karna hai...." Shivani said being tensed.

" Mai doh insaano ko jaanti hu...aur mujhe yakeen hai...wo log madad karange..." Santosh said confidently.

" Toh bula lo......aur yaad rakhna kisi ko bhi khabar nhi honi chahiye...." Shivani warned.

" Aap chinta matt kijiye...kisi ko kuch pata nhi chalega..." Santosh said firmly.

Officers

A uthor's POV

It was now the next day.The birds chirping bringing positive vibes along. The sun today was warm calming the environment.

The villagers of Chakoragao were busy in there morning rituals.Some of the ladies were on their way to fetch water from the well while some were busy putting rangoli in their yard.The men were grooming themselves for the day while the kids were getting ready for their Vidyalaya.The atmosphere was all happy and cheerful.____

" Doctor se baat hui...? " A restlessely walking Santosh asked Shivani.

" Nai abhi doctor kuch jawab nhi de rahe...Tu chinta mat kar... Sab thik hoga" Shivani assured her.

" Kaise chinta na karu...Wo sab zindagi aur maut ke liye lad rahe hai... Mai unhe khona nhi chahtii.." Santosh said her eyes being teared up.

" Tu shaant hoja pehle...aur ye bata wo unn officers ka kya hua...Wo aarahe hai na..." Shivani asked.

" Wo aarahe hai...aajayenge thodi der mein.." Santosh said.

" Tune mission ke secrecy ke baare mein bata diya na...Kisi ko bhi ye pata chalna nhi chahiye ki sab yaha hai..." Shivani spoke seriously.

" Ha maine bata diya hai...hum kar sakte hai un par vishwaas..." Santosh said.

"Mai mil sakti hu unse...Dekhna hai mujhe un sabko.." Santosh further added.

Shivani nodded & took Ss in.

"Mai aati hu...thodi der mein.." Shivani said & left.

Author's POV

As Santosh entered the room the nurse left to give her some privacy.She swiftly moved in and halted. Her eyes teared up again instantly. She wiped her tears and moved towards the first bed._____

" Billu ji...uthiye na...Dekhiye Santosh aayi hai.... Dekhiye wo wali duty chodi maine...Yaha Humare Mahila Police Thane mein agayi mai... Uthiye Billu ji....Aapko cheetah aur meri shaadi dekhni hai na...Uthiye na...billu ji..."Santosh said in between her cries.

" Karishma madam...aap bhi aise kaise so gayi...uthiye na...apni santu ko aise akele kaun chodta hai.... Uthiye jaldi aapka bhaukaal bhi dekhna hai sabko... Hume pata lagana hai na ki humare thane ko kisne jalaya uthiye karishma madam...aur aap mujhe maasi nhi bana aengi...Mujhe khelna hai mere bhatiji aur bhatije ke saath chaliye..." Santosh cried.

" Pushpee....Dekhiye na sab mujhe akela chod gye...Aap toh uthiye na...H um dono ko chugli bhi toh karni hai na..Uthiye....Agar aap uth gayi na toh dekhna sab uth jayenge...mujhe pata hai...aaap sabko jaga dengi..." Santosh longed for her best friend Pushpee

" Madam sir....aap toh jaag jaiye....Dekhiye aap ke kehne par mai chali gyi thi transfer leke par....maine sunni na aapki baat...toh aapko bhi sunna na hoga....Uthiye chali ye hume chaat bhi khaani hai...aur bohot cases bhi solve karne hai...Aur iss baar aap kitna bhi kahe mai mpt chodkar nhi jaungi... Uthiye na madam sir..." Santosh said leaning on Haseena's chest.

" Cheete...dekh teri Santuji aayi hai....Uth na...Mai tujse bohot naraz hu... Ek baar bhi call nhi kiya na tune...Yaad nhi aati thi meri...kitna miss karti thi tujhe...aur jab tu mere paas nhi tha na tab meri maasoomiyat bhi nhi nikal rahi thi ...chal uth ab bol uff ye massumiyat santuji...mai karishma madam ko samjha dungi...wo nhi maregi tujhe...humari shaadi bhi toh baaki hai na.. Chal uth ab bohot hua...Aur uss din bhi mai tujhe mile bina chali gyi...par mai bohot jaldi mein thi...isiliye aur iss baat bilkul nhi jaungi tujhe chod kar.." Santosh said taking Cheetah's hand in hers.

" Sambhal khudko Santosh... Chal bahar doctor aagaye hai unhe check up karna hai sabka..." Shivani said and Santosh outside._____

" Shivani wo Officers agayr hai...Kya kahu unhe kaha bulao..." Santosh informed about the arrival of the officers.

" Chal tu bhi mere saath leke aate hai...unhe...Thoda tujhe bhi accha lagega ". Shivani said.

Author's POV

Shivani and Santosh reached the railway station in the outskirts of Chakor-agao covering themselves with a scarf to maitain secrecy.The railway station was crowded enough...Annoucements about the train's arrival & depature were heard.The people were in a hurry to catch their train in time.There were tempting food stall for the passengers.And their aroma covering the entire railway station.The coolies were roaming here & there for satisfying there daily needs by working.

" Kaha hai wo log...dekh dikhayi dete hai kya..." Shivani said.

" Ha wo rahe..." Santosh said waving a hand at them.

Author's POV

A well built handsome man with great physique dressed in cyan tshirt & blue jean,smiled seeing Santosh and removed his shades.Beside him was a lady officer with a dimpled smile on her face dressed in a yellow short kurta with blue floral prints on it & a blue plaazo. She removed her shades & looked here & there chewing her favorite paan.

" Chal jaldi..." Shivani said & both went.

" Jai hind sir...jai hind madam...." Santosh saluted.

" Jai hind " The both officers saluted her back.

" Chaliye pehle hum ghar chalte yaha safe nhi hai hum..." Shivani said and all got in car.

"Waise aap...?" One of the officer questioned Shivani who was driving.

" Mai Adv.Shivani Pawar....bass yahi samaj lijiye ki bohot ghera naata hai mera mpt se.. Aur aap..?" Shivani answered the officer's question and questioned him back.

" Mai SHO Amar Vidrohi...pehle mahile police thane mein hi tha...Bohot lambi aur atarangi kahani hai humari...Filhal Mumbai mai Sho hu..." Amar introduced himself and Santosh chuckled at one of his statement.

" Hum toh mil hi chuke hai..." The another officer spoke.

"Ji kya maara tha aapne uss din gundo ko...Tabse mai fan ban gyi hu aapki..." Shivani said smilingly while driving.

" Mishri Pandey hai hum...fan toh bante hi hai sab humare...kyu Amar Vidrohi ji..." Mishri said partially looking at Shivani and then giving a flirtatious look to Amar.

" Waise Santosh kuch pata chala...uss hadse ke baare mein..." Amar escaped from Mishri's flirt smartly.

" Nai sir abhi kuch pata nhi chala hai..." Santosh said sadly.

" Tum chinta mat karo Santosh hum pata lenge..." Mishri assured.

Soon they reached Shivani's Vada.

" Aap ko agar aaram karna ho toh side wala room khali hai..." Shivani politely said.

" Nai...ab toh aaram tab hi hoga...jab sab criminal pakde jayenge..." Amar said in determined tone.

" Ji...Amar Vidrohi ji....bilkul sahi keh rahe hai.." Mishri again flirted.

" Toh saaman rakh dijiye..." Shivani said.

"Ji..Waise shaam tak aur ek officer aanewale hai..." Amar said.

" Lekin sir..." Santosh was about to speak.

"Chinta mat kijiye....Bohot acche dost hai humare.. Kuch leak nhi hoga. ..Aur waise humne unhe yaha sirf aane ko kaha hai...unhe bomb blast ke baare mein kuch nhi pata...."Amar confidently said.

" Toh thik hai location bhej deti hu mai aapko aap unhe forward kar dena...Shaam ko bohot log hote hai bahaar...toh safe nhi hai jaana ....." Shivani spoke.

"Ji sure.." Amar agreed.

" Wo dusri wali bohot mithi mithi baate kar rhi thi Amar Sir se...kuch hai kya dono ke beech...?" Shivani questioned Santosh as Amar & Mishri went to their rooms.

" Dono ke beech nhi... Ek tarafa..Mishri madam ko bohot jyaada wala crush hai Amar sir pe...Aur Amar sir bhav bhi nhi dete unhe.."

"Woh toh saaf dikhayi de raha hai..." Shivani chuckled.

"Shaam ko senior doctor aanewale hai...wahi sabki tabiyat ke baare mein batayenge..." Shivani said.

"Hope ki sab thik ho..." Santosh said and hugged Shivani.

Author's POV

Mishri & Amar went to the room where their team mates were kept.As expected the both pairs of the eyes welled up seeing the patriots.Officer Mishri stumbled & disbalanced but Amar quickly holded her arm and blinked assuring her.________

" Jisne bhi haal kiya hai na inka....ek ek ko chun ke maregi ye Mishri Pandey..." Mishri said wiping her tears with an angry voice.

" Chalo...bhaukaali devi ki kami nhi pata legagi..." Shivani said as she saw the same attitude in Mishri & everyone chuckled.

The team is increasing day by day. From only Shivani to Shivani,Santosh,Mishri & Amar. Two people are yet to come.Binni & a officer introduced by Amar.

Who is the new officer introduced by Amar?

How will Binni react to Cheetah & Santosh's relation?

To know keep reading.

Do vote & comment.

"Remember votes & comments, motivate me to write the next part early "

" Votes & Comments are key to early & interesting updates "

~ Kishaaa

The Amazement

Author's POV

The sun was setting in the west leaving a fairy like shade of pink purple whereas the sun was dipped in yellow just like a smiley ball. The kids were enjoying their evening plays. The ladies engrossed in their chit-chat. While the men were working in farms.

~ Patil Vada ~

".Shivani...kab tak aagaye doctor 7 baj gaye hai...aajana chahiye na unhe..." Santosh asked restlessly

" Aree...shaant hoja...aate honge doctor..." Shivani calmed her.

" Aap kabse yhi bol rahi hai..mai kaise shaant ho jau.." Santosh said in a little bit of irritated way.

" Sach mein aajana chahiye doctor ko...bohot der hogayi hai..." Amar too took Santosh's side.

" Lagata hai aagaye..." Mishri said as the doorbell rang.

" Ab toh hoja shaant...aagaye hai doctor..." Shivani said to a restless Santosh and went to open the door.

" Aap kaun...? " Shivani asked looking from head to toes as she noticed a unknown face.

" Hum...wo hume Amar ne yaha bulaya tha... Kisi mission ke liye..." The person said taking of his glasses.

" Shivani....andar le aao na doctor ko..." Santosh yelled before Shivani could react.

The person squinted his eyes as he heard a familiar voice.

" Doctor nahi hai santu...." Shivani said.

"Toh kaun hai..." Santosh said getting up and going towards the door.

Author's POV

As Santosh approaches the door. She's awestrucked to see the person. The awestrucked Santosh stands then & there numb looking towards the person.A person dressed in brown shirt paired with blue jeans with a smiling face then,was now stood at the door with a shocked face.Both, the person & Santosh were looking at each other preparing questions to ask.As it was taking time Amar & Mishri too went towards the door.Mishri was too shocked to see the person but not as shocked as Santosh.Amar smiled seeing the person.________

" Ye...wahi officer hai...jinke baare mein maine bola tha..." Amar said breaking the uncanny silence.

" Ye nhi hosakta...." Santosh whispered.

" Kya nhi hosakta....tu thik hai...rang kyu udd gaya hai tera..." Shivani said in a concerned tone.

" Aap Anubhav Singh hai na..?" Mishri asked.

" Ha ye wahi hai...Aap janti hai inhe...?" Amar questioned.

Author's POV

Mishri glanced at Santosh as she got to know the reason behind her reac
tion.Santosh was teary.While Shivani & Amar stood completely confused
at her reaction.The next moment was a surprising moment for everyon
e.Santosh quickly hugged Anubhav leaving everyone including Anubhav
dumbstrucked.___________

" Mujhe pata tha....aap aisa kuch kar hi nhi sakte...Aap hero hai mere...kuch
galat kar hi nhi sakte.." Santosh said breaking the hug & in between her
sobs.

" Aap the kaha itne din...pata hai sab aapko miss karte the...." Santosh
continued.

" Madam sir toh bohot tut hui thi....bass bahar se hasti thi..." Santosh spoke.

" Kyu chale gye aap....kyu aisa kiya...aapko pata hai mujhe yakeen nhi hua
tha ki aap deshdrohi hai....isiliye maine phirse research shuru ki thi...Dek
hiye aur mai sahi thi...kuch nhi hua hai aapko...." Santosh cried and hugged
Anubhav again

" Shaant hojaiye...." Anubhav said taking her in hug and caressing her hairs.

" Dekhiye..un sab ne kya halat bana rakhi hai...apni....ab aap hi unhe...
jaga sakte hai...chaliye..." Santosh said dragging As with his wrist leaving
Mishri,Amar & Shivani confused.

Author's POV

As Santosh dragged a confused Anubhav towards the room,Anubhav just
followed her.As they entered the room.As had the same reaction as every-

one who witnessed the scene.He was not able to think anything.His mind went blank.He had never imagined this state of his family members.Who can imagine this...no one!He glanced at his sister who was lying on bed with her oxygen mask & medical equipments attached.He further saw towards his lady love and something sharp pierced his heart.Anubhav wanted to broke down the moment but he glanced at Santosh who was looking at him with trust & hope filled eyes.He knew he needs to be calm,as at the moment Santosh is the one who needs to be kept strong.___________

"

Doctor aagaye hai....Unhe check up karna hai.." Shivani informed.

"Ji....chaliye Santosh sharma..." Anubhav said wiping his tears.

" Kaise hua ye sab..." Anubhav asked after being sitted.

Santosh narrated the heartbreaking incident amd how they were safely brought at Chakoragao.

" Kisne kiya... kuch khabar..." Anubhav asked controlling his emotions.

" Filhaal kuch saboot nhi lage hai haat...Crime location se bhi kuch nhi mila hai..." Amar provided with the information he knew.

" Hume lagta hai hume phirse ek baar MPT mein investigation karni chahiye..." Anubhav suggested.

" Ji sir... Par agar hum mein se koi jayega toh pata chal jayega ki koi hai joh investigation kar raha hai..." Mishri stated the fact.

" Uske baare mein hum sochte hai kuch..." Anubhav said.

"Mera shak Devalpar ke unn bhaiyo par hai jinka case chal raha tha....kyu nki ussi case ke baad hi ye sab hua hai....pata nhi kyu par ye sab connected hai..." Shivani said.

" Ha...wo mantri bhi bohot asani se mangaye the jab madam sir ne waha thana khulwane ki baat kari thi...mujhe uss wakt thoda shak hua tha..." Santosh said.

" Jald se jald unn sabko hosh aana chahiye...wahi hai joh hume aage bada sakte hai..."Anubhav said in stressed mood.

" Kaisi hai un sabki tabiyat..." Anubhav asked as doctor was done with checkup.

" Woh thik hai na...? " Santosh asked.

" Ji...2 patients ki jaan ko jyaada khatra hai..." Doctor said tensing the atmosphere.

"Kaun...?" Mishri asked.

" Karishma singh aur cheetah chaturvedi..." Doctor said.

" Mere khyaal se Karishma singh ko asthama ki bimari hai..." Doctor asked
.

" Ji hai unhe Asthama..." Anubhav said.

"Isiliye dhue ke karan unke lungs par bohot gehra asar pada hai..." Doctor said leaving everyone sad

" Aur rahi baat cheetah ki ...toh lagta hai ki wo bomb ke bohot kareeb khade the...isiliye unke body bohot jal gayi hai..." Doctor gave another sad news.

" Wo...wo thik toh hojayenge na..." Anubhav asked trying to be strong.

" To be honest...aapko ummid nhi rakhni chahiye...chances bohot kam hai...phir bhi doctor hone ke naate hum puri koshish karenge..." Doctor said breaking everyone's heart.

" Kuch nhi hoga cheetah aur karishma madam ko....wo jarur thik honge..."
Santosh yelled at the doctor.

" Mai kal phir aauga check up ke liye... I have some doubts regarding the
report...just ek confirmation chahiye.... Aap strong rahiye..." Doctor said
giving them some strength.

" Aur patients baat karte rahiye...wo respond toh nhi kar sakte par aapko
sunn sakte hai...increase their will power with your talks...Ye unke recover
hone ke liye bohot jaruri hai..." Doctor suggested.

" Ji doctor...Thank you" Shivani thanked & doctor left.

" Hum mil aate hai unse..." Anubhav said avoiding eye contact & left to the
room.

" Doctor ne kaha na...hume himmat nhi harni hai... Wo thik hojayenge..."
Shivani consoled a crying Santosh.

" Pata hai...kuch nhi hoga unhe...wo sab phir thik honge..." Santosh said
wiping her tears.

" Waise Anubhav aap sab ko kaise jaante hai..." Amar asked after confirm-
ing that Santosh was fine.

"Wo...Anubhav sir...karishma madam ke bade bhai hai.." Santosh told the
truth.

" Aur madam sir aur wo,dono ek dusre se pyaar karte hai....Sagai bhi hone
wali thi par shayad unki kismat mein milna likha hi nhi hai...Anubhav sir
ko sagai wale din hi mission pe jaana pada...phir jab aaye tab ye mission
behroopiya wala drama hua...bohot dukh sahe hai madam sir aur Anubhav
sir ne..." Santosh narrated.

" Kuch bhi hojaye saccha pyaar humesha jeetta hai " Shivani stated the fact.

"Ha iss bar koi un dono ko dur nhi karega..." Mishri too agreed.

" Aisa hi ho..." Santosh crossed her fingers.

The Loss

Author's POV

Soon all were done with their dinner just to fuel there body for the upcoming challenges.Anubhav who went to the room after the doctor's departure had till now shown no sign of coming out.He talked to every unconscious person present there as doctor instructed to.But no one showed the sign of consciousness.He was now broken but he had to be strong to find out culprit behind the condition of his loved ones.He kept his head on Haseena's bed taking her hands into his.Thinking about some or the other plan to investigate at the crime location that is MPT without giving any clue to the doers of this act.________

" Haseenaji...humne bohot soch liya...ab aapki baari hai..aap hi bataiye kisse bheje hum... Kuch soch nhi pa rahe hum..." Anubhav said kissing her dorsel side palm.

Author's POV

As if universe answered him on behalf of Haseena.Anubhav got his a nswer.He quickly rushed outside with his phone.As he reached the hall Santosh quickly tried to give him a plate full of food.But he denied as the thought he thought was more important to be accomplished.He moved to the terrace.The cool night breeze calmed him down signalling that all will fine super soon.He dialled a number and spoke the needed.And ended a call with his evergreen smile.He felt a hand on his shoulder.He turned to find Santosh there.___________

" Sir mujhe pata hai ki aapko kuch idea aaya hai... " Santosh said the truth.

" Aisa kuch nhi hai... " Anubhav lied

" Aap jhoot bol rahe hai....aap aur madam sir bilkul same to same hai...jab bhi aapko koi idea aata hai aap dono hi ek badi si smile dete ho...bataiye kya idea hai..." Santosh said.

" Bohot acche se jaani lagi hai aap hume..." Anubhav said with a slightly smile face.

" Ha toh aapko hero,idol,bh...kya kuch nhi mana hai..." Santosh said avoiding to say the last word.

" Last mein kya bola aapne..." Anubhav said raising his eyebrow.

" Maine...kuch bhi toh nhi..." Santosh lied.

" Gale nhi lagengi behna..." Anubhav said widing his hands for Santosh to hug.

Santosh shockingly smiled and hugged Anubhav.

" Ab bataiye..kya idea hai..Anu bhaiya..." Santosh said with a chuckle.

" Hume woh officer mil gaya hai..jise hum mpt bhejenge..." Anubhav said.

" Kaun hai wo..." Santosh questioned.

" Mira...humne order de diya hai...wo nikal bhi gyi hogi...kal aajayegi wo reports ke saath..." Anubhav said confidently.

" Mira...Sir aap jante hai mira ne kya kiya hai...wo tin ka dabba phirse kuch gad bad kardega..." Santosh said angrily.

" Anu bhaiya se sir.....aap shaant hojaiye..mira ka software ab update ho chuka hai...kuch gadbad nhi hogi..." Anubhav said.

" Thik hai...Aap kehte isiliye..." Santosh calmed down.

"Ab chaliye niche...aapne khaana bhi nhi khaya hai.." Santosh said holding his wrist.

" Ruk jaiye yaha accha lag raha hai..thodi der baad chalte hai..." Anubhav said and Santosh stood beside him.____________

" Kya baat hai badi acchi lag rhi ho aaj..." Amar said hugging shivani from back.

" Ye wakt hai ye sab karne ka...chodo koi aa jayega.." Shivani said blushing.

(Readers ko laga jor ka jhatka)

(Aaya na maza..?)

"Chod toh nhi sakte..bhagwaan bhi hume alag nhi rakhna chahte...isiliye bhej diya mujhe tumhare paas..." Amar said.

" Wo mishri aajayegi...chodo.. " Shivani said.

"Uska naam kyu le liya yaar...Humesha flirt karti rehti hai... Pata hai.mu mbai se kaise aaya hu mai....chipko hai ekdam.." Amar chided.

"Pyaar karti hai wo tumse.." Shivani said with a not so sweet smile.

" Accha..par mai toh nhi karta na..mai toh tumse pyaar karta hu..." Amar said kissing Shivani's forehead.

" Ha ab chodo aur usse dur rehna..nai toh ye shivani pawar usse chodegi nai..." Shivani warned.

" Mujhe koi khushi nai milti uske paas rehkar..." Amar said.

" Abhi chalo...chodo... Aur ha humare Relationship ke baare mein kisiko nhi batana jab tak mission nhi hojata..." Shivani said.

" Utni akal hai mujmein..." Amar said.

" Akal hai toh jaake so jao...10.30 hogaye hai..." Shivani said and left for her room._______________

Author's POV

The next day had already begun.All were waiting outside as the doctor was doing his work inside.And as told he was going to clear the doubt which was left unsolved.Everyone was very tensed outside gaining power to face whatever comes their way.The doctor arrived._________

" Aap karishma singh ke bhai hai..? " Doctor asked.

" Ha hum...wo thik hai na.." Anubhav asked.

" Aap aasakte hai humare saath...akele mai baat karni hai.." Doctor asked to which Anubhav grew tense.

" Nai..aap yhi bataiye...sab pariwaar jaise hi hai..." Anubhav said controlling the roller coaster inside.

" Unki shaadi ho chuki thi..?"Doctor asked.

" Ha...par kyu.." Anubhav asked confusingly.

" I am sorry to tell but wo iss accident se pehle pregnant thi...Unka miscarriage hogaya hai..." Doctor told to which everyone were shocked.

"Ye kya bol rahe hai...aap.." Santosh said after digesting the news.

" Ji...aur sabse mushkil baat ye hai ki unhe pata tha... Mujhe unki blood reports se tablets ke ansh mile hai...Ho sakta hai doctor ne unhe prescribe kiye ho..." Doctor again sounded bad.

" Abhi unhe hosh bhi aajaye toh...aapko unhe sambhalna hai...wo nhi seh payegi aapne bacche ko khone ka dard..." Doctor continued.

Author's POV

Anubhav sat down with a thud. Santosh sat beside him to console him.E veryone whether close or not to Karishma weren't able to digest the news .The doctor left as he was done with his work.Now it were the only people who will have to console Karishma regarding the news.______________

" Ab hum kaise samjhayenge behna ko...Unhe pata nhi hota toh thik tha hum unhe nhi batate.. Par wo khud janti thi...wo kaise sahegi ye sab.." Anubhav emotionally said.

" Hum haina...Mai hu..Shivani hai Amar sir hai...mishri madam hai...hum sab milke sambhal lenge unhe...aap chinta mat kijite...aapko strong rehna hai...Agar Karishma madam ke Anu bhaiya aise royenge toh unhe kaun sambhalega...aur madam sir bhi toh thik hojayengi...wo haina unhe samb-halne ke liye..." The little Santosh consoled her elder brother.

" Unhone bohot intezaar kiya tha iss pal ka...aur ye sab aise hogaya..." Anubhav said thinking when Karishma longed for a baby.

"Shaant hojao Anubhav...Hum sab milkar sambhal lenge unhe.. " Amar consoled his best friend.

Anubhav looked at all them present there and they shared a group hug.

Loving the brother sister bond between Santosh & Haseena?

What was your reaction on Amar-Shivani as a couple?

How will karishma react on her biggest loss?

To know keep reading.

Do vote & comment.

"Remember votes & comments, motivate me to write the next part early "

" Votes & Comments are key to early & interesting updates "

~ Kishaaa

Everything is Good

I didn't get a proper response on previous part.Hence the reason of late part.Aren't you not liking the story or it's getting boring let me know please!

To my genuine readers " Happy Reading"

Author's POV

About a month had been passed since Shivani saved the MPT members.S till there was no positive sign from the patriots.This only 1 month felt like an eternity for their loved ones.Karishma's health was deteriorating rapidl y.While Cheetah slipped into Coma..Haseena,Billu,Pushpaji were fine but unfortunately unconscious.Anubhav and Santosh were with them every moment talking to them.But nothing worked.In Karishma's case doctor had declared that nothing less than a miracle can save her.Doctor felt that Karishma has sensed the loss of her baby hence does not want to live her life.Binni had too arrived a few days ago.She fortunately got to know about Santosh and Cheetah's relationship through Binni.And positively she accepted that. Mishri had to return back to thana to continue her duty as there was a as usual shortage of police officers._______

" Sir 1 mahina hogaya hai...abhi tak hum kuch nhk kar paye hai...." Santosh sad with pale face.

" Sir aapne toh kissi officer ko bheja tha crime location par...uska kya hua.." Amar asked Anubhav.

" Bheja toh tha..par ab woh humse connect nhi ho parahi hai..." Anubhav talked in frustration.

" Abhi kaun ho sakta hai..." Shivani said as the door bell rang.

" Hoshiyaar rehkar kholna.." Amar said.

Shivani carefully opened the door.

" Kaun chahiye aapko.." Shivani asked.

" Kaun hai..." Anubhav said and went near the door.

" Shivani...mira hai ye...andar aao mira..." Anubhav calmly let her in.

" Mira madam...aap kaha thi...anubhav sir ne bheja tha an aapko mpt toh aap kaha thi pichle ek mahine se..." Santosh questioned.

" I am sorry...Santosh Sharma...Mujhe research time lag gaya..." Mira answered in her robotic ascent.

" Aapko kuch mila hai...?" Anubhav asked.

" Ji...mila hai..." Mira answered.

" Kya mila hai..." Amar asked.

" Sorry mai aapko nhi jaanti..." Mira denied.

" Mira ye humare saath iss mission pe kaam karenge...aap bata sakti hai..." Anubhav said.

" Mujhe ye locket mila hai..." Mira said handing a mysterious necklace to Anubhav.

" Aur kuch..." Santosh asked.

" Ye shoes..." Mira said handling over a pair of shoes.

" Aise shoes kaun chodke jata hai.." Santosh said being confused.

" Sach mein ajib baat hai...shoes kaun chodke jayega...." Amar agreed.

" Aur kuch pata laga mira...?" Anubhav asked.

" Ji nhi sir..." Mira denied.

" Aap ja sakti hai..." Anubhav said.

" Sir...isse bhejna thik rahega...? " Santosh asked Anubhav.

" Don't worry Santosh Sharma... Aapki information mere paas safe hai..." Mira said in her robotic accent.

" Thik hai..." Santosh said and Mira left

Author's POV

After few hours Anubhav was in patient room talking with his loved one's .Whilr Santosh was on terrace calming herself with nature'd magic.Shivani was cooking their lunch while Amar was busy trying to collect some more clue for mission.________

" Akele kyu khadi hai...? " Binni asked Santosh as she to went on terrace.

" Kuch nhi aise hi..." Santosh said.

Santosh ignored Binni a lot as she got to know about Cheetah's relationship with her. She felt a little bad but ignored.The thing that mattered the most now was the recovery of her dearest people and finding the culprit.

" Manne lagta hai...hume humare bich ki misunderstanding ko khatam kardena chahiye..." Binni said seriously but didn't receive any reply from Santosh.

" Tu pyaar karti hai na cheete mera matlab cheetah se..." Binni said correcting herself.

" Meri rai kaun lena chahega... Tum aur cheetah acche lagte ho saath mein..." Santosh's brain spoke hurtfully rather than heart.

" Aisa kyu bol rahi hai...aisa kuch nhi hai..." Binni spoke.

" Toh..tum karti ho na cheetah se pyaar... Date kiyaa hai na tumne ek dusre ko...." Santosh said fuming a little in anger .

" Aree aisa manne lagta tha...par wo pyaar na tha...wo bas ek atraction tha.." Binni said what she felt.

" Thike hai maan leti hu tumhare liye attraction hai...par cheetah agar tumse pyaar karta hoga toh...?" Santosh doubted.

" Nahi karta wo mujhse pyaar...wo bass tere jaane ke baad akela pada tha isiliye ye sab hua..." Binni said.

" Sach mein...? " Santosh said hopefully.

" Ha mai jhoot nhi bol rhi... " Binni said holding Santosh from shoulders.

" Thik hai...tum kehti ho toh..." Santosh said.

" Toh ab manne dost maan le..." Binni said forwading her hand for a handshake.

" Friends.." Santosh said with smile.

" Chal ab niche...jiji ne khana bana liya hai..." Binni said.

Author's POV

After their lunch Anubhav along with Amar were out somewhere re-garding the mission.While Santosh was sleeping near Haseena holding her hands.All others being busy in their work.___________

" Kabse ro rahi thi...abhi jaake soyi hai..." Shivani said seeing a tired crying Santosh sleeping near Haseena.

" Sach mein jiji in sab rishta kitna ghera hai...Khoon ka nhi hai phir bhi kitne jude hue hai sab ek dusre se..." Binni adored the bond.

" Tabhj toh kehte dil ka rishta sabse ghera hota hai...bas ab ye sab thik hojaye..." Shivani prayed.

" Hmm..." Binni agreed.

Author's POV

As Santosh was sleeping she felt something moving on her cheek which disturbed her.She tiredly opened her eyes.Only to find Haseena's finger moving.Santosh forgetting her headache which was due to her crying got up happily tears of happiness making her way._______

" Madam sir uthiye dekhiye...aap thik hai.." Santosh said cheering Haseena.

" Shivani Anubhav sir dekhiye madam sir ne abhj ungli hilayi...wo thik ho rahi hai..." Santosh yelled happily.

" Sach mein..." Shivani asked coming running.

" Ha dekho..." Santosh said showing haseena's moving finger.

Binni entered with the doctor who co- incidentally came for the check up.

" Aap sab bahar wait kijiye..." Doctor said & everyone went outside.

Santosh tried calling Anubhav and Amar a lot but their phone was un-reachable.

" Ye phone kyu nhi utha re dono..." Santosh chided.

" Aajayenge...shaant raho...." Shivani said.

After sometime doctor after his checkup called everyone in.

" Inki health ab stable hai...aajayega hosh ab inhe..." Doctor said about Haseena's health.

" Aur lagta hai ki aapki baate sab par asar kar rhi hai... Karishma aur cheetah ke bhi chance bad gaye thik hone ke... Keep going " Doctor said with a smile and left.

" Madam sir sunna aapne aap thik hai karishma madam aur cheetah bhi jaldi thik hojayenge..." Santosh cheered Haseena.

" Uthiye na madam sir..." Santosh pleaded.

Author's POV

As Santosh pleaded Haseena started getting her senses back.Santosh hopefully looked at Haseena.While Shivani & Binni stood there.The trio laughed in joy seeing haseena back in her senses.________

Haseena's POV

I felt someone speaking to me and this time it wasn't unclear like before.I could hear the voice & words clearly.I tried once to open my eyes but they were too heavy to open and my head started paining.So i gave up again but again i heard the same voice .I tried once again and I was successful at it.I couldn't see any anything clear.The scene before me was blurred.All i could see was someone's unclear face.I tightly closed my eyes and again opened to find a girl no...a fair n lovely girl before me.After few seconds I found that it was SantoshShe was smiling like mad with her tearful eyes.Wait...Why was she here and what happened to me...?Why am I feeling that i have woken up from a long sleep.I tried to speak but my mouth hurts.I am unable to open my lips to talk.Tears make their place in corner of my eyes.__________

" Aap thik hai...?" Santosh asked taking Haseena's hands into her.

Haseena just nodded her head up & down as words weren't ready to escape her mouth.

"Madam sir boliye..na..." Santosh cried.

The tears stuck at corner of Haseena's eyes flowed down.

" Wo bol nhi paa rahi hai..thoda sabar kar.."Shivani said to Santosh.

Haseena tilted her eyeballs to find Shivani & Binni there.Haseena again focused back to Santosh and made a confused face.

" Aapko kuch bhi yaad nhi hai..." Santosh asked to which Haseena nodded no.

" Humare thane mein...bl...blast hua tha...phir shivani ne aap sab ko yaha laya..." Santosh told the incident in a shivering voice

Author's POV

Haseena tilted her head with great difficulty.Tears again made their place in the corner but denied to fall.Haseena remembered the incident and was givjng hundred percent to control her emotions.This is when Anubhav & Amar entered in hurriedly.____________

" Aap baar call kyu kar rhi thi Santosh...sab thik hai..." Anubhav asked as soon as he entered in.

Everything is getting good now!

How will Haseena react seeing Anubhav?

To know keep reading.

Do vote & comment.

"Remember votes & comments, motivate me to write the next part early "

" Votes & Comments are key to early & interesting updates "

~ Kishaaa

Haseena

A ap baar call kyu kar rhi thi Santosh...sab thik hai..." Anubhav asked as soon as he entered in.

Haseena's POV

As i opened my eyes with great difficulty I found Santosh,Shivani,Binni infront of me.Next what i heard shocked me.I heard a deep husky familiar voice.I turned my eyeballs towards the room entrance.I group of mixed emotions took over me.He was standing before me...Anubhav was standing fit & fine before me.He looked at me and was shocked.For the first time i noticed some tears in his eyes.____________

Author's POV

As Haseena Anubhav looked at each other both the pair of eyes welled up.Both were just staring at each other.

A murmur escaped from Haseena's mouth." Anu...Anubhav".A first word after her second birth.Indeed it was a second birth..who can still be alive after such a huge bomb blast.

Shivani,Santosh,Amar & Binni left the room to give them some privacy.

Anubhav walked towards her with slow steps.He sat down on a chair placed beside the bed.

Haseena's tearful eyes now gave up.Tears started oozing out.Amd pretty soon turned into sobs.

Anubhav wiped own's tears and caressed his hand from Haseena's forehead to her hairs.

New tears were making their way down Haseena's voice.Anubhav wiped her tears lovingly.____________

Haseena's POV

I want to hug him badly.I want to ask him why he left me alone at the time i needed him the most.

But i wasn't able to speak a single word nor i was able to move my body to hug him.____________

Author's POV

Anubhav placed loving kiss on Haseena's forehead to which Haseena closed her eyes feeling peace.

Next thing was which Haseena wanted.Anubhav hugged her still in the sleeping position.With great difficulty Haseena lifted both her hands and hugged him lightly.________________

" Hum jante hai.....Aapko bohot sawaal puchne hai...par aap chinta mat k ijiye...aab jo chahe wo puch sakti hai...par pehle acche se thik hojaiye...hum hai aapke paas..." Anubhav said breaking the hug & cupping her face.

Haseena gave light positive nod with tears still in her eyes.

" Abhi chup hojaiye...bilkul aashru nhi chahiye hume aapke aankho se..."
Anubhav clamed her wiping her tears.

Haseena turned her neck to the side where MPT members were and again
turned towards Anubhav asking him through her eyes.

" Sab thik hai....bas behna..." Anubhav was about to tell but stopped realising that she should not have any mental tension.

Haseena squinted her eyes asking what happened to Karishma with fear
visible in her eyes.

" Kuch nhi wo bhi thik hai...Aap aaraam kijiye jaldi se thik hona hai na
aapko...." Anubhav said and put a comforter over her.

Haseena wasn't at all satisfied with the answer but gave up as she wasn't
able speak.

" Hum aapke liye khana late hai..." Anubhav said & escaped as he was
controlling his emotions.___________________

" Jabtak Haseenaji thik nhi hojati tab tak unhe behna ki halat ke baare mein
koi nai batayega...." Anubhav warned everyone.

" Sir ye madam sir ka dinner hai...khila dijiye..unhe dawai bhi leni hai...."
Santosh said handing him the plate.

" Aur doctor ne kaha hai ki unhe dusre room meim shift karde... Unhe
better feel hoga..." Amar added.

" Ji...khana khane ke baad..." Anubhav said and got back to Haseena.

____

" Chaliye hum aagaye aapka dinner leke uthiye...." Anubhav said placing
her plate on the chair and helping her to sit straight.

" Chaliye muh kholiye...." Anubhav instructed.

Haseena opened her mouth slightly and Anubhav fed her first morsel.

Tears again formed there place in her eyes.

" Mat roiyye haseenaji...sab thik hojayega.." Anubhav calmed.

" Aap baat karne ki koshish kariye.... Aise chup acchi nhi lagti aap..." Anubhav said feeding her the next morsel.

" Aap...thik...hai...? " Haseena suceeded at speaking.

" Kuch bhi puchti hai aap..Hume aapko puchna chahiye ki aap thik hai..." Anubhav said.

"Abhi chaliye dawaiya le lijiye...." Anubhav said handling her two tablets.

Haseena silently gluped the tablets.

" Doctor ne aapko dusre kamre shift karne ko bola hai...ab se aap humare saath rahengii..." Anubhav said.

Haseena looked at MPT members.

" Wo bhi jaldi thik hojayenge..." Anubhav said.

Author's POV

Anubhav carefully made Haseena stand by holding her shoulders.And took her to his room .Santosh joined helping Anubhav.Both had held her from either side.Haseena was very thankful to be alive.___________

" Aap thik hai na madam sir...?" An emotional Santosh questioned.

"Ha hum thik hai..." Haseena answered noticing her emotions.

" Gale nhi lagengi santu..." Haseena asked spreading her hands.

Santosh hugged her and haseena kissed her.

"Kya re jazbaat wali bai..ghabra ke chodiya humko..." Shivani said

"Thank you hum sabko bachane ke liye.." Haseena said.

" Thank you mat bol....dost hi toh dosto ke kaam aate hai..." Shivani said while tapping her cheek.

"Waise Amar vidrohi aapko bhi thank you" Haseena said.

"Uski koi jarurat nhi hai.....wo kya haina dushman ko kuch hojaye toh hume maza nhi aata...." Amar said.

" Aap abhi bhi nhi badle na Amar " Haseena said little bit informally.

A tinch of jealousy sparked Anubhav on seeing Haseena friendly with Amar.

" Santosh Haseenaji ko change karne mein madat kardo.... Hum hai bah ar.." Anubhav said

Anubhav went to do his daily routine i.e talking to Karishma and everyone who are not still recovered.

Soon Santosh helped Haseena changing her clothes.

" Sir madam sir ne kapde change kar liye hai...bass ye cream unki burns par lagana hai...wo mana kar rhi hai..." Santosh said handing over the tube to Anubhav.

" Hum dekh lenge..." Anubhav said taking the tube.

" Haseena ji aaiye hum ye laga dete hai..." Anubhav said coming towards Haseena.

" Nai...humne baaki jagah laga liya hai...hume chehre par nhi lagana...bo hot jalan hoti hai...." Haseena denied.

"Kuch jalan nhi hogi hum haina hum lagate hai...Aaiye..." Anubhav said making her lie on bed.

Author's POV

Anubhav took some cream on his fingers.He carefully started applying it on Haseena's burns.Haseena closed her eyes due to pain.After applying enough amount.Anubhav began blowing air to calm Haseena's pain.Ha seena soon opened her eyes as she was relieved.

Both shared a eyelock for a moment.Anubhav broked the eye contact & lied himself beside Haseena.

Both were just staring at the ceiling.Anubhav closed his eyes in tiredness .But Haseena was getting flashbacks of the incidents happened there and her near & dear mpt members condition.

" Sojaiye...Wo sab thik Hojayenge....aur hum uss insaan ko bhi pakad lenge jisne ye kiya.." Anubhav said carefully taking her into his arms & not hurting her wounds.

" Good night " Haseena snuggled into him.

" Shubh ratri priye.." Anubhav replied.

Haseena blushed hearing her special name from her special person.

Everything is great going between Anuseena!

Wondering what is the truth of mission behroopiya?

How is Haseena friendly with Anubhav after mission behroopiya..?

To know keep reading.

Do vote & comment.

"Remember votes & comments, motivate me to write the next part early "

" Votes & Comments are key to early & interesting updates "

~ Kishaaa

Pushpee

Author's POV

It was a new morning after the night Haseena recovered.All were were happy to see Haseena all okay but tensed for the other ones.All except Haseena were having there morning tea sitting in the courtyard.Haseena was strictly warned by the doctor for complete bed rest.

"

Kya pata laga hai..." Anubhav asked Amar.

" Do logo ke fingerprints mile hai...Forensic bhej diye hai...pata chal jaye ga..." Amar answered.

"Thane mein exactly kya hua tha woh toh madam sir hi bata sakti hai..." Santosh exclaimed.

" Par unse abhi yeh puchna thik nhi...doctor ne mana kiya hai koi bhi mansik dabaav dalne ke liye..." Anubhav sadly said.

" Udhar ke cctv bhi damage hue hai...usse bhi kuch pata chalne se raha..." Santosh said a little irritated.

" Bas wo fingerprints hi hume untak pohocha sakte hai..." Shivani said.

Author's POV

After their tea time,Anubhav departed to Haseena to wake her up.While Santosh went to do her daily routine i.e talking with her loved ones.____

____

" Chaliye abhi kiske thik hone ki baari hai..." Santosh said entering the room.

" Karishma madam...chaliye uthiye...dekhiye madam sir thik hogayii hai. .." Santosh said sitting beside Karishma.

"Aapko milna nhi unse...? Phir hume saath milke dhoondna bhi haina criminals ko..." Santosh said taking Karishma's hands into hers.

" Koi nai aapko aur sona hai...so lijiye lekin jaldi thik hojaiye.." Santosh said with shivering voice but hopeful tune.

" Cheete tu toh uth ja....bohot daatna hai mujhe tujhe...chal na cheete date pe chalte hai...tu kabse keh raha tha par mein nhi sunti thi na...chal ab mein khud keh rhi hu..." Santosh said moving towards Santosh.

" Billu ji...uthiye na aap...aap agar cheete ko nithale kahenge na...toh wo jarur jaag jayega..." Santosh said now with tears in her eyes.

" Pushpee...aise akele kaun chodta hai apni best friend ko...aapko pata hai...madam sir aur anubhav sir ek saath hai...hume unki shaadi bhi toh karani hai....uthiye...." Santosh said leaning on pushpa's chest.

It worked Pushpaji's machine started beeping.

Santosh lifted her head and looked towards the machine.

She hurriedly called everyone inside.

" Lagta hai...inhe hosh aaraha hai..." Amar said examining the monitor as he was medically trained.

" Pushpee...thank you meri baat sunne ke liye...chaliyve uthiye..." Santosh started cheering.

" Kya hua...sab thik hai....?" Anubhav hurriedly entered as he was busy making Haseena have her breakfast.

" Sir...pushpa ji ko hosh aaraha hai..." Santosh hugged Anubhav happily.

" mubarak ho...aapko aapki saheli wapas mil gayii..." Anubhav said reciprocating the hug.

Author's POV

Pushpa ji was all good now.She tried to open her eyes and was successful at it in the first attempt.Though her vision was blurry yet but her senses were now conscious._______________

" Santu...?" Pushpaji whispered Santu's name as she clearly got the view.

" Shivani....binni...amar sir..." Pushpaji said being confusion.

"Ye sab humare saath hai...jisne bhi ye blast kiya haina unhe sab milke pakadenge..." Santosh explained which made Pushpaji recall the past happenings.

Author's POV

The big blast....the fire was all Pushpaji was remembering.Then she remembered her partners she had a view looking at each side of her seeing them.On looking at Karishma her eyes welled up instantly as she got a clue.The welled up eyes hence proved that Pushpaji does know about the good news which wasn't good now.She again tilted her head back at Santosh.Asking her about Karishma's health.Santosh unable to answer left the room without glancing at her.This was the time Anubhav came before Pushpaji.She was shocked to the core to see him.She was happy yet sad yet confused.______________

" Hum thik hai...aur baaki ki kahani aapko baad mein batayenge..." Anubhav said calmly.

" Ka...kar...karishma...." Pushpaji spoke with great difficulty point her saline wired hand towards Karishma.

" N...na..nai..raha...un..unka..baccha...." Anubhav revealed with a great difficulty.

The next moment Pushpaji broked into tears.Anubhav hugged her calming her down.

" Aap shaant rahiye...Aapbhi ko sambhalna hai unhe...aap kamzor nhi pad sakti..." Anubhav said while Amar,Binni,Shivani were teary.____________

Soon Pushpaji was shifted to Shivani's room as it was mandatory to be with them 24/7.

Anubhav had informed Haseena about Pushpaji's recovery.Hence she asked to meet her.Anubhav was determined to tell about Karishma's baby to Haseena today.

" Hum aapse kuch kehne wale hai...par aap wada kariye ki aap jyada mann ko nhi lagayenhi..." Anubhav warned Haseena.

"Aisa kya batane wale hai aap..." Haseena asked confused.

"Wo....behna..." Anubhav stopped ad it was difficult for him.

" Karishma singh...unhe kya hua wo thik hai...? " Haseena started overthinking.

" Behna thik hai...par..." Anubhav tried to continue.

"Par...kya...?" Haseena asked.

" Wo...blast ke pehle garbhavati thi...un...unka miscarriage hua hai... " Anubhav finally said.

" Unka...baby....!" Haseena said recovering from the shock.

"Aap jyada havvi matt hoiye...aap hi hai joh unhe sambhal payengi..." Anubhav said caressing Haseena's hairs.

" Hum thik hai.. " Haseena said wiping her tears.

Anubhav took Haseena to Shivani's room by supporting her by one side as she was unable to walk solely

Haseena & Pushpaji were emotional seeing each other.

"Aap thik hai...?" Pushpaji asked carresing Haseena's cheek.

Haseena nodded positively with tears in her eyes.

Haseena's attention drew towards Santosh who was asleep on Pushpaji's lap just like a child who met her mother after a long time.Everyone adored them.

" Pata hai...humari bahurani bohot khush thi...khabar ko lekar..." Pushpaji said.

" Wo batane wali thi....thane ke function ke baad aap sabko...par ye sab hogaya..." Pushpaji said wiping her tears.

" Bohot intezaar kiya tha...humari bahurani ne iss pal ka...kaise lag raha hoga bechari ko...Har din shiv mandir jaakar prashad chadhati thi.." Push-paji said reminiscing the old memories of Karishma wishing a baby.

" Anubhav sir..ho sake toh humare lalla ko yaha bula lijiye wahi ek hai joh unhe sambhal payega..." Pushpaji requested.

" Ha...hum karte hai kuch..." Anubhav said wiping his tears.

———————

Humari pyaari Pushpee is super okay now !!!

Will Anubhav get a idea to bring Lalla to Chakorgao without letting the criminals get hint..?

To know keep reading.

Do vote & comment.

"Remember votes & comments, motivate me to write the next part early "

" Votes & Comments are key to early & interesting updates "

~ Kishaaa

Mystery

A uthor's POV

15 days passed since Puspaji & Haseena's recovery. Haseena and Pushpaji had narrated all the happenings before the blast to the members yet they were clueless of what to do! The non recovery of Cheetah Karishma and Billu were adding more restlessness to them. Now Pushpaji and Haseena were too the addition to talk to the MPT members everyday. P uspaji was luckily all okay although she had some scars but they weren't severe. Haseena still had the bruises over face and hands. Anubhav took her care not less than a baby._____________

" Sir, Aap batane Wale the...mission behroopiya ka raaz ... Bataiye na abh i..." Santosh pleaded.

" Ha sir bata dijiye...kabse soch rahe hai kya hua tha uss mission mein..." Pushpaji added.

" Vaise mujhe bhi Janna hai...kya hai ye mission behroopiya " Amar to showed interest.

" Manne laage hai bohot kuch chinna hai ye mission ne aapse..." Binni said reading their faces.

" Ha mujhe bhi yhi lagta hai...dekh iss jazbaat wali Bai ka chehra kitna utar Gaya hai..." Shivani said looking at Haseena.

" Aap sab itna keh hi rahe hai toh suniye....". Anubhav started.

Flashback.

Haseena lifelessly lying in bushes down the mountains.Her body covered with lots of blood.Blood still oozing out her stomach and chest,pain all visible in her eyes.She had no power left to shout for help too.

Anubhav the saviour luckily got to know about the trap and hence found his lady love covered in a pool of blood.Anubhav took her to urgent medication.Of course! At his secret place as going to hospital wasn't safe at all.He took proper care of her till she fully recovered.On the other side at MPT all were mourning about Haseena's death.Karishma was broken no one could fix that.Santosh and Cheetah were helpless.Billu mistakened it as joke but soon got out of it.Pushpaji was hurt too but alone strong to console her children.

Here,with Anubhav 's care Haseena was all okay.____________

" Aapko humara saath dena hoga..." Anubhav said to Haseena.

"Hum aapka pura saath denge ..." Haseena agreed

"Hume 99% Shak hai bakshi sir hi wo gunhegaar hai... jinhone Mira ko hack Kiya..bas humare paas saboot nhi hai...aur court humse saboot man gega... isiliye aap wahi kahengi joh bakshi sir kahenge..." Anubhav narrated his plan.

Author's POV

Anubhav informed Karishma about the same but later on his entry on 26 January.Karishma was emotional but agreed she also got to the truth of Urmila.And mission continued.

On the last day of the mission where Karishma and Haseena shot Anubhav with bullets he wasn't injured.The bullet proof jacket saved him.The whole area was under CCTV surveillance hence each and every minute moment was being recorded.

After falsely shooting Anubhav, Karishma took Haseena to the hospital as she was injured badly and unconscious,this was not a part of plan.Anubhav had mistakenly hurted Haseena to which he was too guilty.Haseena was good after her medical treatment in minutesHere as soon as Haseena's treatment was done both reached the prior location.

Bakshi was restlessly searching for the pendrive.Anubhav was continuing the plan he was still acting to be lifeless.

Haseena and Karishma hid behind a big bar present there witnessing the whole situation.

When they knew the recording was enough to prove Bakshi criminal in court they entered the ground clapping their hands to which Bakshi turned towards them.

Anubhav taking it as a sign got up and stood behind Bakshi.Bakshi looked at both of them shockingly.

" Amaa aapka zindagi se sambandh kharab hua kya... Karishma Singh ko chakhma dedoge..." Karishma shouted in anger.

" Toh aakhir pata chal hi Gaya tumhe sach..." Bakshi smirked.

" Bohot kuch pata chal hai sir ...itna ki aapki sir kehne mein bhi sharam aarahi hai.." Haseena said in anger.

" Kuch nhi bigad paogi tum dono mera...mai pendrive haasil karke rahu nga..." Bakshi challenged.

" Toh dhundiye kaha hai pendrive...." Karishma said.

" Pendrive nai bhi mila toh koi gam nai...Iss deshbhakt ko mar Diya yhi kaafi hai mere liye ..." Bakshi said as he still didn't know about Anubhav being alive.

" Toh sir chaliye court chalte hai..." Haseena said coming forward.

" Kanoon ko saboot chahiye hote hai...hai tumhare paas mere khilaf sabo ot....?" Bakshi asked.

" Ek nhi sir 6- 6 saboot hai...ye dekhiye ye hai humare paas " Karishma said showing the video captured through CCTV

Bakshi's step reversed.He was walking back towards Anubhav.Thud! His back got hitted with a muscular chest.He turned only to be shocked.

" Tum Zinda ho...?" Bakshi questioned in scared tone.

" Kyu ..aapko koi vipatti..." Anubhav said holding him from his neck.

" Chaliye aapko aapke shi jagah par pohochane ka wakt aagaya hai..." Anubhav threw him in police Jeep and the constable and an IB officer took him to lockup.

" Aap thik hai...Haseenaji..." Anubhav instantly questioned Haseena.

" Ha hum thik hai..." Haseena nodded.

" Ab aap dono ko koi nhi Durr kar sakta..." Karishma said with a smile.

The trio sighed a relief and shared a hug.

" Abhi Hume jaana hoga...aap dono humare baare mein kisi ko bhi nhi batayengi..." Anubhav said placing either of his hand on Haseena and Karishma's shoulder.

" Laut jaldi aana...Ab intezaar nhi hoga humse.." Was all both could speak.

Anubhav smiled and left.Haseena and Karishma too left happily to MPT.

Flashback Ends.

" Bakshi sir Aisa kar sakte hai humne socha bhi nhi tha..." Pushpaji spoke teary.

" Mujhe toh unse pehle se hi nafrat thi...humesha madam sir ko aur Anubhav sir ko alag karte hai..." Santosh chided.

" Mai toh nhi jaanti...ye kaun ...par ye accha hai ki tum log thik ho...". Shivani said happily.

Everyone's attention drew towards Haseena who was sleeping leaning on Anubhav's shoulder.

" Ye toh so gai..." Anubhav chuckled looking at her.

" Humne sach mein aaj tak inka ye roop kabhi bhi nhi dekha..." Amar said looking at carefree Haseena.

" Sir...aap le jaiye madam sir ko andar..." Pushpaji said doing the signature evil eye step.

" Ha..." Anubhav said picking her up in arms.

He placed her on bed,tugged her in her blanket and pecked her forehead and returned to the room where all were sitting.

" Sir...lalla ka kya hua ...kuch hua hai .." Pushpaji asked.

" Ji ...humne unhe unknown mail bheja hai...Doctor ki jarurat toh Hume bhi hai ...toh ussi bahane wo yaha aajayenge...Kal aajayenge wo.." Anubhav assured Pushpaji.

" Jaldi se lalla aajaye..." Pushpaji prayed joining her hands.

" Shivani aur Amar aap dono hi Jaana unhe laane..." Anubhav said and both nodded.

" Ye Santosh kaha gyi..." Binni said looking around.

" Woh andar hogi ..." Shivani said looking at the closed door of the room where Cheetah Billu Karishma were kept.

" Kuch bhi hojaye...humara Cheetah jaldi se thik hojaye....santu kitni badal gyi...hai...na uska wo bachpana dikhta hai na uski maasumiyat...." Pushpaji emotionally spoke.

" Baate bhi bohot Kam karne lagi hai wo...." Anubhav added.

" Tum sab chinta na Karo...sab thik hoga..." Binni assured.____________

____

The day ended with their talks.

Talks with a tinch of negativity but ample of positivity and hope.

Santosh decided to spend her night near her love Cheetah.

Everyone were just manifesting to get a clue to the bomb blast and recovery of their loved ones.

Good Night!!!

The mission behroopiya, isn't a suspense anymore!!!

How will Lalla react seeing his mom and wife?

To know keep reading" THE AFTERMATH "

Do vote & comment.

"Remember votes & comments, motivate me to write the next part early "

" Votes & Comments are key to early & interesting updates "

~ Kishaaa

Cheetah

- -

Author's POV

The rising of the sun, chirping of the birds signalled the beginning of a new day.The climate out was a little cold and more fresh bringing a healthy and positive atmosphere everywhere.

It was a happy day for Pushpaji but tensed too !!Her dear son was going to arrive today.She was tensed about how will he react seeing them here as he didn't know why was he called here!!Moreover how will react seeing his wife whom he loved madly in an unimaginable state.And what about the loss of their baby!!!____________

" Utho na bahurani...lalla aayega toh hum kya kahenge usee...." Pushpaji said caressing Karishma's hair.

" Ae bille tu hi bol na kuch ulta sidha....Tab hi toh ye tujhe kantaap Marne ke liye uthegi...." Pushpaji said emotionally looking at Billu.

" Santu ki bhi halat kaisi Hui hai....Cheetah ko chod hi nhi rahi..." Pushpaji said looking at Santosh who was still sleeping with her head on his chest.

"Ae Santu uth subah hogayi hai...Aise soyegi toh gardan akad jayegi..." Pushpaji said moving towards her tapping dear daughter's cheek lovingly.

Santu woke up from her slumber..Adjusting her eyes to the morning light she opened her eyes finally!She glanced at Cheetah and just smiled and got up.

Author's POV

"Beep...Beep...Beep" The machine attached to Cheetah started making noises.Of course we find the noise irritating but to our MPT members the sound was sweet as honey.

Santosh and Pushpaji turned towards the machine.Santosh screamed joy ously.Hearing the voice Anubhav and Amar entered.___________

" Amar sir dekhiye cheetah ki machine awaaz kar Rahi hai...Usse hosh aaraha hai..." Santosh exclaimed joyously.

" Ha...inhe bhi hosh aaraha hai..." Amar said with a wide smile.

"Dekha ... Pushpaji mai kal raat cheete ke paas thi iska asar hai ye...." Santosh said hugging Pushpaji.

" Ha ha ..santu...hum bohot khush hai..." Pushpaji said caressing her back.

Till now Haseena,Binni and Shivani arrived and were happy with scene.

Author's POV

Cheetah's eyes finally twinkled.Creases formed on his forehead.Here, Santosh's cheering was continuosly going on at a higher pace.Cheetah with a great difficulty opened his eyes.Ceiling was the first thing he looked at.He further moved his eye balls down that is towards Santosh.He was awestrucked.___________

"Sa...sa...ssantuji..." He murmured weakly.

" Ha cheete Teri santuji ....dekh yaha sab hai... Pushpaji...Madam sir...A mar sir.. Shivani ...Binni..Aur dekh Anubhav sir bhi hai..." Santosh said showing everyone wiping her tears.

Cheetah looked at everybody he was ofcourse shocked at Anubhav's pres ence.But everyone calmed him down._____________

" Aap aaram kariye...aapko hum shaanti se sabkuch batayenge ...." Anub-hav answered his unasked question.

"Mai tere liye khana lati hu..." Santosh said and ran outside.

Cheetah was shifted to Santosh's room.

" Anubhav sir...lalla ka koi message aaya...?" Pushpaji said to Anubhav.

" Aajayenge thodi der mein" Anubhav said sadly._

____

" Chal cheete jaldi khale ... Tujhe dawai bhi Leni hai..." Santosh said feeding him a morsel.

Cheetah was just looking at Santosh.

" Mai Teri dawaiya leke aati hu..." Santosh said leaving with the plate.

As Cheetah felt thirsty he tried to grab a glass full of water from the table near his bed.

But Alas!! His fractured hand didn't allow him to do that...Binni was passing by the room she noticed this and instantly entered and gave him the glass.

" Dekh mai jaanti hu...tu Santosh se pyaar kare hai ...Mai na aaungi tum dono ke beech... Aese ghur mat mujhe... Dosti toh nai kharab karte hum ..." Binni said with a smile.

" Shukriya " Cheetah said.

Meanwhile Santosh arrived.

" Ye le dawaiya .." Santosh said giving him tablets.

" Cheete tujhe pata hai mai aur binni bohot acche dost ban gaye hai...." Santosh said making him drink water.

"Bataya binni ne..." Cheetah said.

" Chalo ab Mai chalti hu...tum dono Karo baate ...."Binni said and exited

" Naraz hai aap humse..." Cheetah asked Santu.

" Nai...mai tujhse naraz kyu hongi..." Santosh denied.

" Binni ki vajah se ..." Cheetah said.

" Tu abhi bhi ussi baare mein soch raha...chod wo hum dono misunderstandings thi wo clear kardi hai....Ab kuch mat soch..." Santosh said applying the ointment on his wounds.

" Thank you Santuji...." Cheetah thanked.

" Ye kiss liye..." Santosh asked.

" Aap laut ke aagayi isiliye..." Cheetah answered

" Tum sabki Jaan khatre mein ho aur mein wapas na aau aisa hosakta hai bhala ..." Santosh said with a smile.

" Billa aur Karishma madam bass jaldi se thik hojayee ..." Cheetah prayed

" Tum sab thik ho toh woh dono bhi thik hojayenge .." Santosh said positively

Author's POV

A handsome man dressed in a formal look sitting in a compartment of a train.The man seemed sad and was looking out of the window probably for some peace.As the train stopped he took out his locket from his pocket and kissed the picture placed in the locket.____________

" Tum dono ka sapna tha na ki tum dono Desh ki seva karni hai....toh wo sapna mein pura karunga... Naraz toh main tum dono se hu... Akele joh chod gaye mujhe...par koi nai...aaj yaha kisi police logo ki madat karne aaya hu... " The person said looking at the picture in his locket.

The person wiped the only tear from his eyes and took his luggage and got down from the train.

He dialled a number and soon conversation ended.__________

" Woh aagaye hai...aap dono jaiye...par kisi ko bhanak bhi nhi lagni chahi ye...." Anubhav warned Amar and Shivani.

"Ji aap chinta mat kijiye .." Shivani and Amar said at a time.____________

Amar and Shivani reached the station and were finding the person.Amar pointed towards the person to which Shivani nodded positively.

They approached the person.

" Aap Shivani aur Amar ...?" The person asked.

"Ji ...aapko hi pick karne aaye hai ..." Amar said.

"Ji ... Chaliye..." The person lifted his bags and started walking.

" Aree uncle rukiye...aapka locket gir gaya ..." A little girl came running from behind.

" Oh... thank you... ye lo tumhara inaam .. ye mere liye bohot kimti hai " The person handed her a chocolate.

Amar and Shivani smiled as they noticed the picture in the locket .

(Humare readers toh hai hi hoshiyaar)

" Thank you..." The girl said with a smile.

" Tu yaha kya kar rahi hi...ka wapas wo log dhund rahe honge..." Shivani warned the girl.

" Ha ha rahi hu....mujhe jara bhaji-pav khane ka man hua isiliye yaha aayi thi ..jahi rhi hu..." The girl answered Shivani.

" Chaliye...." Shivani said and the trio headed towards the car.

" Waise aap...? " Amar asked while Shivani was driving.

" Myself Mihir Singh....mera hospital hai Dubai mein par abhi kuch reasons ki vajah se permanently India shift hua hu...." The person,Mihir said.

Soon they reached the Pawar Vada.

Shivani rang the bell to which Anubhav opened the door...

Finally Cheetah is alright now!!There's no misunderstanding between Santosh,Binni and Cheetah.

How will Mihir Pushpaji ka Lalla react seeing Anubhav?

And what about Pushpaji and Karishma!!

Will Mihir's presence help Karishma to regain her life?

To know keep reading" THE AFTERMATH "

Do vote & comment.

"Remember votes & comments, motivate me to write the next part early "

" Votes & Comments are key to early & interesting updates "

~ Kishaaa

Lalla

S hivani rang the bell to which Anubhav opened the door...

Author's POV

The opening of the door made a roller coaster of emotions on Mihir's face.The bags in his hand fell on the ground with a thud.___________

" Anu...bhav...Aa..aap yaha....Aap thik hai ..." Mihir said in a shivering voice.

" Aap pehle andar aaiye..." Anubhav said holding him from shoulder while Amar and Shivani took his luggage in.

" Aapko...kuch nhi hua....aa...aap hi the jinhone Hume bulaya..yaha..." Mihir asked.

" Ha...hum hi the wo..." Anubhav nodded.

The next moment Mihir could not control and hugged him.

" Aapko pata nhi hi...kya hua hai ....humari Amma aur hamari Karu...hum sabko chodke chali gyi ...." Mihir said in a shivering voice.

" Shaant...jija ...ji...hum aapko kuch batayenge aapko bass Shanti se sunna hai ..." Anubhav said calming him down.

" Aapki Amma aur Karu dono thik hai....unhe kuch nhi hua hai..." Anubhav said

" Aap mazak kar rahe hai....Aree mujhe khud call aaya tha ..... Unke thaane mein blast hua aur koi nai bacha..." Mihir said emotionally.

" Yeh sahi hai ki blast hua tha par unhe kuch nhi hua hai ... Shivani ne unhe bacha liya hai ..." Anubhav said pointing towards Shivani.

" Toh woh thik hai toh kaha hai wo ...Bataiye kaha hai wo... Bohot mushkil se Maine khud ki sambhala hai..." Mihir asked.

" Yahi hai wo dono ....wo dono nhi balki mpt ke sabhi log yahi hai...." Anubhav said.

" Lalla ...." Pushpaji called out Mihir lovingly.

" Ammaa ...." Mihir turned back looking at Pushpaji.

Mihir ran towards his dear mother and hugged her just like a small child hugging his mother.

" Ammaa aap thik hai ....aapko kuch nhi hua..." Mihir said still hugging his mom.

" Hum bilkul thik hai lalla ...filhal tumhari Karu ko tumhari zarurat hai ...." Pushpaji said caressing him

" Karu....Karu thik haina..." Mihir asked.

" Nai hai wo thik... Wo jaag hi nhi rhi....tum ek baar baat karlo....dekho tumhari baato se jaag jayegii ...." Pushpaji said.

" Mujhe milna hai usse...." Mihir said

" Ha ...chalo..." Pushpaji took him to the room.

Author's POV

As Pushpaji took Lalla to the room she left giving him some privacy.Mihir was shocked seeing his lady attached with lots of medical equipments and wires.

He moved towards her and sat on stool beside her.He took her salined hand in his and kissed it with tears present in his eyes.He closed his not allowing the tears to flow out._____________

" Aisa koi karta hai kya karu...Mai aaraha tha na milne tumse...khud itni khushi se mujhe batati ho aur phir aisi halat baba li....chalo utho tumhare patidev aagaye chalo..." Mihir said still kissing her hand.

" Aur tum humare baby ki chinta matt Karo...woh jaha bhi hoga thik hoga... Uske vajah se tum mujhe Amma ko matt chodo...chalo na karu utho ...." Mihir said patting her cheek.

" Ye vahi hai na Billu ....jisse tum roz chidti thi...dekho wo bhi aise hi pada hai...tum utho phir woh bhi uth jayega...." Mihir said looking at Billu.

Mihir sat in same position for a whole one hour.Haseena entered disturbing his thoughts.

" Toh aap hai... Pushpaji ke lalla ...." Haseena said sitting on the either side of Karishma.

" Hmm" Mihir just whispered

" Aap chinta matt kijiye Karishma Singh bilkul thik hojayegi..." Haseena gave him a hope.

" Aap jaisa kahe vaisa hi ho..." Mihir said still looking at Karishma.

" Bohot baate karti hai karu aapke baare mein... Bohot maanti hai aapko..."
Mihir said smiling at Haseena.

" Humari sabse acchi dost hai wo...kyu Karishma Singh ...." Haseena said
looking at Karishma.

" Chaliye bahar Anubhav aapko bula rahe hai..." Haseena said and left.

While Mihir too followed her.___________

" Iss sab ke baare mein kisi ko kuch pata nhi chalna chahiye ..." Anubhav
said to Mihir

" Hum kisi ko kuch nhi pata lagne denge...." Mihir assured.

" Aur aap behna ki chinta mat kariye...wo jaldi thik hojayegi ...." Anubhav
calmed him

" Mai karunga karu ka ilaaj...wo chutkiyo mein thik hojayengi..." Mihir
decided.

" Waise aapko headquarters se call aaya tha...." Anubhav asked.

" Haa... " Mihir nodded.

" Aapko kuch ajeeb laga jab aap Lucknow aaye...? " Anubhav asked.

" Nhi .... ajeeb toh kuch nhi laga...par kyu..." Mihir denied.

" Kyunki abhi tak Hume koi suraag nhi Mila hai ki ye bomb blast kisne
Kiya hai ..." Anubhav answered.

" Sir wo shoes se kuch pata chala..." Santosh asked

" Nai usse bhi kuch pata nhi chala .." Anubhav answered

" Filhaal Shak ke daire mein toh mantriji aur wo devaliya brothers hai...."
Haseena shared her thoughts.

" Agar wo hi hai in sabke piche toh Hume unke khilaaf saboot bhi toh chahiye..." Amar added.

" Saboot waha jaake hi mil payega.. ." Binni said.

" Itni jaldi Hume nhi lagta Hume waha Jana chahiye...iss maamle ko sampurna roop se shant hone dena chahiye..." Anubhav said the fact.

Author's POV

"Beep! Beep" A sound came from the room.Everyone rushed to the room to see what that was!!!

Mihir monitored the machine which beeped and smiled looking at every one.------------------

Just a bonus update as you all were excited for Pushpaji ka Lalla !!!

Guess who's machine it was Billu or Karishma?

Do vote & comment.

" The more votes and comments the more early will be the part uploaded "

~ Kishaaa

Billu

A uthor's POV

On the beeping sound everyone ran towards the room.The machine beeping was Billu's.Mihir quickly checked his vitals and turned to everyone smiling._______________

" Unhe hosh aaraha...!" Mihir said.

Everyone were delighted hearing him.Pushpaji went near Billu and sat beside him.

" Ae bille chal jaldi uth ....dekh humara lalla aaya hai.....tujhe kabse milna tha na usse ...chal ab mil lein..." Pushpaji said

" Ha Billu ji dekhiye....aapka nithalla dost bhi thik hogaya hai...cheete baat kar jaldi se .." Santosh said dragging Cheetah near him

" Ae bille uth na...tujhe mujhe chidhana nai hai kya...." Cheetah said.

"Shrimaan uthiye...hum Anubhav hai uthiye...." Anubhav cheered.

Author's POV

Everyone's cheering helped Billu to get back to life again.He started opening his eyes slowly.It did pain but he gave his hundred percent.

Pushpaji was the first person to whom Billu saw!!Pushpaji giggled happily making Billu smile too.

Billu slowly slightly moved his neck towards everyone seeing them with teary eyes._________________

" M..mai jan...ta tha ki aap kuch galat k...ar hi nhi sakte" Billu said with a great difficulty to Anubhav.

" Shreeman...aaram kijiye aap " Anubhav said smiling.

" Inhe mere kamre shift karte hai..." Amar said.

" Jii...." Anubhav agreed.

" Karishma madam ...kaha...hai..." Billu asked as he didn't find her.

" Aap unki chinta matt kijiye...woh bhi jald hi thik hojayegi...." Mihir answered.

" Pushpaji ye aapka lalla hai na. ....aapke jaisa dikhta hai..." Billu said looking at Mihir.

Billu was shifted to Amar's room the next moment.

The MPT had won the half war already only recovery of Karishma and finding the culprit was the another half to win the war.

" Ab bass behna ko hosh aajaye...phir hum aadhi jang Jeet jayenge ..." Anubhav said looking at the room where Karishma was kept.

" Karishma bhi jaldi thik hojayegi.. maine pehle bhi kaha tha ab bhi keh rahi hu...Chakorgao ki hawa kuch alag hi hai kisi ko jyada din bimar nhi rehne deti...." Shivani stated the fact.

" Toh h Karishma madam ko bahar garden mein rakhna padega .." Santosh said out of innocence.

" Uff ye badi din baad wala masumiyaat....Shivani aise nhi aarahi thi..." Cheetah said in his signature tone.

" Yaha bohot positivity hai...Mai aise aarahi thi..." Shivani explained.

" Cheete abhi toh tune yluff ye masumiyaat bol Diya par Karishma madam ke thik hi hojane pein mat bolna.... control rakhna tho da...." Santosh warned Cheetah while everyone let out a small laugh.

Author's POV

10 days more passed Everyone was too happy seeing their win.Santosh's innocence had returned back now!!Billu's jokes helped everyone spend their day.Everyone wishing for Karishma's recovery was still the same.5 days earlier Karishma had responded to Mihir by holding his hand but that was it,there no other sign of recovery.Everyone still remained positive.

Just a quick short update!!!

Billu is all okay now and back with his jokes !!!

Karishma showed a slight sign of recovery!

Will Mihir's presence help her recover?

To know keep reading

Do vote and comment!!

I know this part is way too shorter than other parts.

I am busy with my studies hence giving shorter updates rather putting it on hold and making you all wait!!

But I promise next one will be longer!!

~

Kishaaa

Ammi

A

uthor's POV

The pale crescent moon shone like a silvery claw in the night sky.The atmosphere was cool than usual.The stars twinkling, setting the perfect night atmosphere._______________

" Dheere dheere sab thik hora hai..." Anubhav said to Haseena who was leaning on his shoulder.

" Hmmm ..." Haseena hummed.

" Jija keh rahe the behna bhi jaldi se thik hojayegi " Anubhav said.

" Hmm.." Haseena hummed again

" Haseenaji...aap thik hai...baat kyu nhi kar rhi.." Anubhav said looking at Haseena downwards.

On recieving no reply again Anubhav lifted her face up.Her ever charming face was gloomy at the moment and a little teary too.

" Aap ro rhi hai..." Anubhav said in tensed tone cupping her face.

Haseena his her face into his chest hugging him tightly.

" Kya hua haseenaji...aap aisi shaant kyu hogayi..." Anubhav said kissing her hairs.

"Aapki tabiyat thik nhi hai ...kuch horaha hai aapko..." Anubhav again asked receiving no reply from her.

Haseena nodded negatively still being snuggled.

" Toh kya hua..." Anubhav asked breaking the hug but Haseena hugged him again looking sideways.

" Bataiye kya hua haseenaji..." Anubhav asked caressing her hairs.

" Am...Am..Ammi ki yaad aarahi hai..." Haseena said with crying puppy face and a tears escaped her eyes.

Anubhav didn't know what to do hence kept caressing her.

" Humne jab Mihir ko dekhna...unki halat dekhi na...tab Hume bohot bura laga..." Haseena said sobbing.

" Humari Ammi ki bhi halat aisi hi hogi...Hume Ammi chahiye Anubhav..." Haseena said like small kid.

" Shaant hojaiyee aap... Ammi thik hai bilkul ..." Anubhav said wiping her tears.

" Kaise thik hogi wo unka Chand ka tukda yaha hai aur unhe pata nhi hai...wo kaise reh rahi hogi humare bina..." Haseena winced.

" Ammi bilkul thik hai...Aapke chacha ji unhe apne ghar le gaye hai...unhe kuch bhi nhi pata hai blast ke baare mein...." Anubhav revealed.

" Par...hume unki bohot yaad aarahi hai ....." Haseena said sadly.

" Hum yaha toh nhi bula sakte na unhe...unki Jaan ko khatra hoga....aap chahti hai aisa ho....? " Anubhav started explaining her like a baby.

Haseena nodded negatively.

" Toh jab Tak hum sab lucknow nhi jaate tab tak Ammi ko wahi aapke chachji ke paas rehne Dena accha hai na..."

" Hmmm...." Haseena agreed.

" Dekha aap ittu sa royi toh aapko bukhaar aagaya...Aap sojaiye hum dawai lekar aate hai..." Anubhav said trying to shift her on bed.

" Nai rehne dijiye ...aap yhi rahiye Hume bohot Darr lag raha hai ...." Haseena said holding his wrist.

" Haseenaji hum thi toh hai...Bass bahar se dawai laarahe hai ...Jija ji ne kaha hai na aapki sehat ko nazar andaaz nhi karsakte..." Anubhav said rubbing her shoulder.

" Nai...aap kisi ko bol dijiye dawai lane ko...hum aapko nhi chodne wale...." Haseena said tightening her grip.

" Accha haat toh chodiye hum Shivani ko bolte hai ...." Anubhav said and Haseena instantly left his hand.

Anubhav called Shivani and asked her to bring the tablet.

As Anubhav ended the call Haseena again held his wrist and snuggled onto him.

" Haseenaji...Shivani aarahi hai room mein...woh aise dekhengi Hume kya sochengi ...." Anubhav said looking at child like Haseena.

" Kuch nhi sochegi wo...sab jante hai....hum dono ek dusre se pyaar karte hai...hum aise hi rahenge...." Haseena said hugging him tightly.

" Aandar aau mai..." Shivani knocked on the door.

" Ji...aaiye..." Anubhav asked her to come in.

" Ye lijiye...." Shivani said giving the tablet to Anubhav.

" Hum paani laate hai...." Anubhav said trying to get out of Haseena's grip.

" Nai ..." Haseena tightened her grip whining.

" Ruko Mai deti hu..." Shivani chuckled looking at them and filled the glass kept on the table with water.

" Ye le..." Shivani gave the glass.

Haseena gulped the medicine and Anubhav made her drink water.

" Mai chalti hu...good night..." Shivani said still adoring the couple.

" Shubh ratri..." Anubhav wished back but Haseena just smiled waving her hand at her.

" Abhi so jaiye kisi bhi cheez ki chinta matt kijiye..." Anubhav said covering her with comforter.

" Hamare Anu..." Haseena kissed his cheek.

" Hamari priye sojaiyye " Anubhav said kissing her cheek.

Soon the couple dozed off in a peaceful sleep in each other's arms.

Who says elders don't long for mother's warmth!!They surely do! So did Haseena

Also some Anuseena moments today!!!

Jazbaati Haseena is ok but childish Haseena hits different!!!

Next part pakka long hoga

Do vote and comment...

Keep reading" THE AFTERMATH "

~ Kishaaa

Karishma

Author's POV

Haseena soon got over from Ammi's emptiness because of the love Anubhav and others gave her.The case hadn't proceeded yet.Anubhav was waiting for the perfect timing to proceed the case as the criminals may be still alert.Karishma's health showed a little development day by day.This all was possible because of Mihir and everyone who spoke with her daily.__

" Ye dekhiye Hume aaj humare saaman se kya mila..." Anubhav said showing a bundle of old photograph to unconscious Karishma.

" Kitni pyaari thi na aap bachpan mein..." Anubhav said in a teasing manner and got lost into a flashback.

Flashback starts

" Dikhaiye na aur tasveere..." A 13 year Karishma whinned.

" Dikha rahe hai baba ruko..." Anubhav's mother her chachiji said

" Isme bhaiya kaise lag rahe hai ..." Little Karishma laughed seeing her brother dressed like girl in the photograph.

" Jyada hasoo mat behna ..." A 18 year old Anubhav chided.

" Hasse nhi toh kya kare...koi bhi hass padega agar aapki ye photo dekhi toh...." Karishma said again laughing.

" Ye dekho ye tasveer...isme tumne pure kapde hi ulte pehne hai..." Anubhav said showing a photograph where Karishma was dressed in a police uniform but whole inside out.

" Ha toh bass 6 saal ke the hum ...Hume kuch nhi aata tha ..." Karishma said being a little embarassed.

" Toh hum bhi chote hi the..." Anubhav said.

" Par humse toh bade hai na aap..." Karishma again chidded and their banter continued.

" Aree bas karo...kya baccho ki tarah lade ja rahe ho...." Karishma's mom ended their banter.

" Anu tum toh bade ho na tumhe samajna chahiye..." Anubhav's mother scolded him.

" Kya maa aap bhi...humari baju lene wajah unki le rahi hai ..." Anubhav complained.

" Ha toh tu bada hai...bado ko humesha choto ki hisse ki daant sunni chahiye ..." Anubhav's mom said.

" Kuch bhi...." Anubhav ignored and continued looking at the pictures.

" Yeh dekho behna...tum kitni pyaari thi bachpan mein..." Anubhav said showing her a pic.

" Pyaare the matlab...ab nhi hai kya ... Abhi bhi pyaare hai hum... " Karishma said grumpily.

" Lekin Hume toh bachpan wali Karishma hi pyaari lagti hai...." Anubhav again made fun of his sister.

" Hume abhi koi nai rok sakta...." Karishma said standing on the sofa with cushion in her hand in a position to throw at Anubhav.

" Tum dono ka kuch nhi ho sakta...." Maa and Chachiji said in unison and got up to do their chores while Anushma continued their fight.

Flashback Ends

" Aapne sunna nhi humne kya kaha.... Uthiye maariye Hume....humne kaha na Hume choti wali behna hi pasand hai ...." Anubhav said emotionally.

" Yaha toh Chachi ji ya maa bhi nhi hai...Hume daant ne toh aap Hume aaram se maar sakti hai ..." Anubhav said looking at Karishma with hopeful eyes.

" Uthiye behna ....aapne aapke Anu bhaiyaa ko aise akele kyu chod diya,...." Anubhav said with teary eyes.

" Aapko toh kitna pasand hai ye tasveere dekhna...ye dekhiye hum khud dikha rahe hai..." Anubhav said.

" Hume chachiji ne bataya ki aap bohot dhundti thi inn tasveero ko ...kintu hum hi le gaye the inhe humare saath... kyunki har baar humare naa hote hue aap roti thi inhe dekh ke..." Anubhav revealed emotionally.

" Accha woh chodiye....hum aapse wada karte hai..ki hum aapko kabhi bhi bhaiya kehne se nhi rokenge...chahe hum on duty kyu na ho..." Anubhav promised shaking hand with her wired hand.

" Aur hum.... hum aapse ab jidd bhi nhi karenge ki hune mama bana do ... " Anubhav said with a great difficulty.

" Wo shishu jaha bhi hoga surakshit hoga....woh kabhi nhi chahega ki unki maa aise kharab halat mein rahe ...." Anubhav said.

This worked!!!After a minute or two Karishma's machine started beeping.

" Jija ji jaldi aaiye..." Anubhav said shouting joyously calling Mihir.

Everyone entered.

" Dekhiye behna ka machine bhi awaaz kar raha hai...." Anubhav happily exclaimed.

" Hume dekhne doh..." Mihir said hoping for best.

" Karu tum thik ho...utho karu....dekho sab tumhara intezar kar rahe hai ...." Mihir said leaning at the height of Karishma's bed.

Everyone were sheding tears of happiness.

" Karu utho...." Mihir said lovingly adjusting the oxygen level of her mask as she started breathing heavily.

" Hume bahar wait karna chahiye ..." Haseena said sensing the situation.

Everyone exited the room.

" Karu utho..." Mihir motivated.

Author's POV

Karishma started breathing heavily as seconds passed.Mihir grew tensed with is heartbeat increasing with her breath.

He caressed Karishma hairs to calm her down.Next he rubbed her feet to maintain the body temperature.

Soon Karishma was calming down.She calmed down now!!

Mihir wiped her face covered in sweat with a napkin gently.

Here outside everyone just praying for her recovery.

Karishma started trying to open her eyes.Adjusting to the sunlight was a difficult task for her as been in como for months.

Karishma opened her eyes adjusting to the sunlight.Mihir got to her forehead and kissed lovingly.Karishma just looked at Mihir blankly.Mihir was smiling in tears while Karishma was still sinking into the moment._____

______

" Karu ...itna pareshaan karta hai kya koi..." Mihir said hugging her lightly.

" K...ka ..un ha...hai...aa ...aap..." Karishma asked with shivering voice.

" Karu tum aapne patidev ko bhul gyi ...." Mihir said while Karishma looked confused.

" Ruko Mai baaki sabko bulata hu..." Mihir said getting up and opening the door letting everyone in.

Karishma looked at everybody one by one.

" Behna ..." Anubhav said coming front.

" Ka...kaun ha...hai...aa...ap log...." Karishma panicked.

" Hu...hum...aapke Anu bhaiyaa..." Anubhav said shivering.

" Karishma Singh hum ...hum...madam sir...aapki madam sir...." Haseena coming forward but Karishma stayed blank.

" Aree Hume pehchano....hum aapki Amma...jisse aap roz ladti hai..." Pushpaji said strongly.

" Aree mujhe toh pehchaan...Mai Shivani...Maine tum logo ki kitna pareshaan Kiya tha..." Shivani said.

" Ha aur mai binni mujhe toh pehchaan mein toh Teri tarah bhaukaali hu ...." Binni said

" Humne bhi aapke naak mein dam kar rakha tha ...Amar hai hum ..." Amar said.

" Tum sab shaant raho...madam mai Billu the spy aapka bestfriend...aap mujhe thapad Marti thi ..." Billu said giving some past hints.

" Ye dekhiye ye nithalla....aap ye ufff maasumiyat bolne par isse bhi karti thi...." Billu said pulling Cheetah forward.

" Ha madam hum Cheetah..." Cheetah said with tears.

" Ha wo mere liye uff ye maasumiyat bolta tha....mein maasumiyat ka bh aandar...aap mujhe singhade khane ke liye bolti thi..mai maasumiyat....aap bhaukaali aur madam sir jazbaat....yaad aaya kuch..." Santosh said already sobbing but this worked.

" Aa....Aah ....!! " Karishma whinned in pain as she felt a sharp pain in her head which made her unconscious.

" Karishma/ Karu/ Karishma Singh" All shouted in fear.

A long part as promised!!

This part came up with some Anushma moments

Why is Karishma blanked out ??

Why isn't she recognising her family?

Will this have a great effect on happiness of her loved ones?

To know keep reading" THE AFTERMATH "

Do vote & comment.

"Remember votes & comments, motivate me to write the next part early "

" Votes & Comments are key to early & interesting updates "

~ Kishaaa

Emotions

" A a....Aah ....!! " Karishma whinned in pain as she felt a sharp pain in her head which made her unconscious.

" Karishma/ Karu/ Karishma Singh" All shouted in fear.

Everyone leaved the room as Mihir asked...He put back the oxygen mask on Karishma which normalised her abnormal breathing.He prepared for a syringe and soon injected it into Karishma's nerves.

" Please karu ..hume bhul mat jana" Mihir said caressing her head and kissed her palm sitting beside her.

A few moments later...

" Aa...Aa.." Karishma winced in pain due to her headache alerting Mihir who resting with his eyes closed.

" Karu..." Mihir left her hand and again caressed her hairs."Pa...patidev..A a....aap ...y...yaha kya kar rahe hai....." Karishma finally recognised him.

Mihir sighed relieved breath.

" Au ..aur hum...hum kaha ...hai..." Karishma said in a panicked tune.

" Tum shaant hojao...Mai tumhe sab batata hu..." Mihir said tapping her cheek.

Karishma closed her eyes for a moment trying to recall the past evil scenes.

"Hum...hu...humara...ba...baccha..." Karishma said looking to her left and right and then keeping her hand on her stomach.

Mihir was gathering words to speak.

" Hu...Hume kuch mehsoos kyu...nhi ho...horaha..." Karishma said sensing her baby. Yaa! A mother can sense the movements may it be too tiny.

" Ka... karu...." Mihir took her hand in his while Karishma looked scared.

" Hu...Hume ..jaana hai...hum....humara ba...by ake...la ho....hoga..." Karishma said taking her hand out of Mihir's and pulling out the saline wire.

" Kar... karu shaant hojao...." Mihir said holding her tightly.

" Aise kaise aap jaante nhi hai ....wo bohot shaitaan hai ... Chodiye Hume jaane dijiye uske paas ...." Karishma said struggling to get out off Mihir's grip.

" Humara baby chala Gaya Hume chod ke ...." Mihir spoke in shivering tone.

" Accha....ye sapna hai...rukiye hune jaagne dijiye....Hume humare bacche se koi sapne mein bhi Durr nhi kar sakta...." Karishma refused to believed in reality.

This was breaking Mihir's heart into pieces...It was enough!!Mihir gripped Karishma's shoulder and shaked her to get her out of shock.

" Karishma...." Mihir roared shaking Karishma.

Karishma looked at him blankly.

" Yeh sach hai ....woh nhi Raha ab..." Mihir said cupping her face and brusted into tears.

Karishma looked at him and her stored tears started falling down.

Mihir joined his forehead to her's and both had a emotional breakdown.

" Humare saath hi kyu... hota hai ye ....kyu Hume ye Khushi nhi milti...." Karishma said in between her sobs.

" Karu shaant tumhari tabiyat thik nhi hai shaant hojao. .." Mihir said carefully laying her on bed.

He wiped his own tears and Karishma's carefully without hurting her burns.

" Kyu hua humare saath aisa ..." Karishma whinned again.

" Shayad bhagwan ko ye manzoor nhi tha karu....humare haath mein kuch nhi tha ..." Mihir said still wiping her tears.

" Bhagwaan aise kaise kar sakte hai...kyu ek bacche ko apne maa se Durr karte hai..." Karishma complained.

" Kyunki....shayad unhe sab dikhta hai joh hume na dikhta ho..." Mihir said deep words.

" Humne ...kitne sapne dekhe the ... Sab toot gye ..." Karishma said remembering the life she dreamt after having a baby.

" Aisa ...thodi tut sakte hai.... Hum phir se try karenge na ... Pehle Hume tumhari sehat par dhyaan dena hoga ...." Mihir tried to explain.

" Hmm" Was all from Karishma's side.

" Pushpaji...madam sir ...cheetah ..Billu....wo kaha hai ...woh kyu nhi dikh rahe ....thik hai na woh ..." Karishma again panicked.

" Ha wo thik hai....mein bulata hu unhe...." Mihir said going out.

Everyone except Anubhav enters the room.

" Humari bacchi ..." Pushpaji ran and hugged her ofcourse tears flowing from both the pairs of eyes.

" Tum kisi bhi cheez ki chinta matt Karo... hum tumhe kuch nhi bolenge...." Pushpaji said cupping her cheeks and Karishma instantly hugged her mom breaking it after few good seconds.

" Aa...aap thik...hai..." Haseena said moving forward controlling her tears.

" Hmm" Karishma rested herself in Haseena's hug as Haseena hugged her.

" Aisa dobara matt karna...hum humari dost ko nhi kho sakte..." Haseena said while tears flowed down.

" Hmmm..." Karishma said breaking the hug.

" Sachmein....madam aapne hum sabko dara diya tha..." Cheetah said.

" Ha Mai bhi akele hogaya tha...koi nhi tha jhagda karne....na thapad maarne..." Billu said while everyone giggled but Karishma just smiled.

" Aap teeno yaha ..." Karishma asked looking at Shivani Binni Amar.

" Saviour... Shivani humari saviour hai... Aur ye log humari madat karenge case solve karne mein.. " Santosh said coming in front as she was hiding behind Amar.

" Sa....santu . ..tum...yaha..." Karishma questioned.

" Ha toh mere pariwar ko meri jarurat ho aur Mai na aao...Aisa kaise hosakta hai bhala ...." Santosh said smiling with tears while Karishma replied with a smile.

" Humse milne ki kisi ko rucchi hi nhi hai..." Anubhav said opening the door and moving towards Karishma with frown.

" A...Anu bhaiyaa..." Karishma whispered with tears.

Anubhav embraced his sister pecking her forehead.

" Aap thik hai....aapko kuch nhi hua..." Karishma said looking at him from head to toes.

Karishma looked at him and again hugged him seeingba smiling Haseena from the gap of his hands.

" Abhi bohot hogaya milna jhulna aur rona dhona... abhi aap aaram kari ye...." Anubhav said breaking the hug while Karishma nodded.

Anubhav made Karishma lay on bed and covered her with a comforter.

Everyone smiled seeing the brother sister duo and left the room.

Anubhav took left the room giving privacy to Mihir and Karishma.

" Kaisa laga sabse milke..." Mihir asked caressing her hairs.

" Bohot accha...." Karishma said with a smile.

" Aaram karo... thodi der hum tumhe dusre kamre mein le jayenge...hm m..." Mihir said kissing her forehead.

" Hmmm." Karishma hummed.

Hushh!!! Karishma got her memory back

Karishma is much affected by loss of her baby!!

How will her loved ones help her come out of the bitter truth?

To know keep reading" THE AFTERMATH "

Do vote & comment.

"Remember votes & comments, motivate me to write the next part early "

" Votes & Comments are key to early & interesting updates "

~ Kishaaa

Buddy

Author's POV

Days passedKarishma was now shifted with Mihir.She was not yet completely out of the shock but everyone tried to distract her from it.She spent her whole in her room with least interaction with everyone making them worry.But who can feel the pain of a mother who just lost her unborn child.No one talked to her about the blast not making her more depressed.At the end Karishma was important than anything.__________

"

Aandar aa sakte hai hum...? " Haseena asked knocking to Karishma who was busy looking out of the window.

" Aaiye na madam sir ...aap aisa kahe puch rhi hai...." Karishma said looking at Haseena.

" Hume laga ki aap busy hai...kuch soch rhi thi kya aap..." Haseena said coming in and sitting on the bed.

" Aaj ...aap khana lekar aayi..." Karishma asked probably changing the topic.

" Ha wo aapke patidev Anubhav ke saath thoda busy hai isiliye hum aaga ye..." Haseena said taking the lunch in her hands.

" Accha ..." Karishma said.

" Aapne humare sawaal ka jawaab nhi diya...kuch soch rhi thi aap .." Haseena didn't forget her question.

" Nai...hum ka sochenge..." Karishma said fakely smiling.

" Hum aapse kal nhi mile hai...pehle se jaante hai aapko... jhoot mat boli ye..." Haseena said in a little stern voice picking a morsel from the plate to feed Karishma.

" Hum kha lenge ..." Karishma said with slight tears in her eyes.

" Kyu...hum khilaye toh kuch hoga kya...accha thike Hume aap senior mat maniye...hum aapki dost hai abhi..." Haseena said smilingly slightly.

Haseena fed her the first morsel and soon the whole lunch.Though it was silent but their eyes spoke a lot.Haseena kept the topic for later avoiding Karishma's breakdown during her lunch.

" Ye lijiye aapki dawai kha lijiye...hum haath dhokar aate hai..." Haseena said forwarding her the tablets and water.

" Ab bataiye kya soch rhi thi aap ..." Haseena said comfortably sitting in front of her.

" Bataiye Karishma Singh..." Haseena said lovingly holding her hand as she hesitated to share her hidden emotions.

" Humne kaha na hum aapki dost hai bataiye ..." Haseena said caressing her hands.

" Hu ..hum naraz hai..." Karishma said.

" Humse....?" Haseen asked confused.

" Nai... khud se...." Karishma said avoiding any eye contact.

" Woh bhala kyu...." Haseena said.

" Aise hi..." Karishma said.

" Agar aap yeh soch rhi hai ki...aapka baby aapki vajah se iss duniya mein nhi raha toh ye galat hai...." Haseena said understanding her untold feelings.

" Dekhiye aapke haato mein kuch nhi tha...joh hua woh sab hona tai tha..." Haseena explained.

" Humara jimmedari tha humare bacche ki dhaal banke uski raksha karn a...hum woh bhi nhi kar paye..." Karishma said slightly teary.

" Karishma Singh...Hume galat matt samaj na... Par abhi joh hua usse badala toh nhi ja sakta na ... Aur rhi baat aapki toh isme aapki koi galati nhi hai...aapko thodi pata tha ki waha blast hoga...nhi na??...toh khud ko kyu kos rhi hai aap...." Haseena said caressing her cheek.

" Aapko pata hai upar wala kuch bhi aise hi nhi karta ..kuch reasons hote ...ho sakta shayad aapke baby ko delivery ke time koi complications aate aur usse takleef hoti...toh kya aap dekh paati kya usse uss takleef mein...nhi na...bass yhi baat hai..." Haseena made her understood.

" Dekhiye hum kisi ki Ammi toh nhi hai ... Aur isiliye aapke puri feelings nhi samaj sakte...bass itna pata hai ki hum humare dost ko takleef mein nhi dekhna chahte..." Haseena said smilingly teary eyed looking towards Karishma.

Karishma threw herself in Haseena's arms crying bitterly.

" Bohot bura hota hai humare saath...." Karishma said in between her sobs

Haseena was just caressing her hairs.

" Aapko pata hai doctor ne kaha kya tha ..." Karishma said breaking the hug.

" Unhe kaha tha ki hum kabhi...pre... pregnant nhi hosakte... phir kaise chamatkaar se Hume ye Khushi mili thi ... Woh bhi nhi tik paayi... isiliye Hume bura lag raha hai..." Karishma said crying.

" Humne Pushpaji ko doctor ki ye baat bilkul nhi batai..." Karishma revealed.

" Aapko unhe batana chahiye tha na ..." Haseena said.

"Agar hum unhe baata dete toh shayad unhe accha nhi lagta...wo humse bura nhi par ajeeb bartaav karti ... hum ye sab nhi chaye the....." Karishma cried.

" Aapko pata hai.... jab aapko promotion Mila tha na tab...hum bohot khush hue the ...ki aur ek khushkhabri sunn kar aap aur khush hojayengi.." Karishma again hugged Haseena.

" Shaant hojaiyee....bohot hua ... Hum bhi chahte the ki aap apni feelings apne andar rakhe isiliye humne ye sab pucha..." Haseena said kissing her over her hairs.

" Thank you ....Hume bohot halka mehsoos hua ...." Karishma said still in the hug.

" Ho sakta hai humara dusra baby aane tak usse koi partner bhi mil jaye uski koi Bhai ya behen uske mama ke baache ..." Karishma said quickly jumping into a teasing mood.

Haseena badly blushed at her statement .

" Kaise laal ho rahi hai aap madam sir ..." Karishma giggled looking at a blush full Haseena while Haseena smiled seeing Karishma back to normal.

" Jabse Anu bhaiyaa aaye hai na tabse hum aapka chehra khil gaya hai... Nazar na Lage.." Karishma said smiling.

" Aapko bhi.. aise hi muskurate rahiye aap..." Haseena said kissing her cheek.

They stayed in the hug for few moments and broke it when they were at peace.

" Hum aasakte hai andar..." Anubhav knocked.

" Aaiye na .... Aap hi ki baat horahi hai..." Karishma said smiling while it felt peace to Anubhav seeing her.

" Aisi kya chugli kar rhi thi aap humare baare mein..." Anubhav said coming in.

" Na...nai kuch nhi...hum aapko baad mein batayenge..." Haseena avoided.

"Aap apne piche kya chupa rahe hai .." Haseena said in order to change the topic.

" Ye behna ke liye hai..." Anubhav replied.

" Humare liye...?" Karishma questioned.

" Ha ye dekhiye...." Anubhav sat down near Karishma.

" Ye photo album toh kho Gaya tha..." Karishma said being shocked.

" Nhi...hum le gaye the ise apne saath ..." Anubhav revealed.

" Hume dekhna hai...." Karishma said.

" Ha toh dekhne ke liye laaye hai...aaiye hum dono dekhte hai..." Anubhav said opening the album.

Haseena escaped living the brother sister duo alone.

" Woh thik hai na...." Pushpaji asked tensed.

" Bilkul thik hai dekhiye..." Haseena said asking Pushpaji to peek through the door.

Pushpaji thanked God instantly.While everyone sighed a relief seeing everything good.

Okay! A Kareena dedicated part today!

The two best buddies indeed nazar !

Everyone is completely fine now!

How will the story take a turn further?

To know keep reading" THE AFTERMATH "

Do vote & comment.

"Remember votes & comments, motivate me to write the next part early "

" Votes & Comments are key to early & interesting updates "

~ Kishaaa

A little start

Ignore any typos if found..Mera keyboard update hogaya hai and I am unable to type with a great speed.Kabhi Karishma likhte likhte Jarishma ban jaata hai

---

" Behna kya keh rhi thi " Anubhav asked after spending his whole day with his sister.

" Kya keh rhi .." Haseena asked confused.

" Aree wo jab hum andar aaye the tab..." Anubhav made her remember.

"Wo ....wo Kuch nhi keh rhi thi..." Haseena said hiding her blush.

" Bataiye na....kya baate chal rhi thi humare baare mein .." Anubhav said.

" Kuch nhi..." Haseena said.

" Aisa kya hai joh aap itna sharma rhi hai..." Anubhav said leaning closer.

" A..aa...aap ye kya kar rahe hai...." Haseena fumbled.

" Aap bataiye pehle nhi toh hum kya karenge dekhiye...' Anubhav said looking towards her lips.

" Anu.... Anubhav.... Hum batate hai..." Haseena said fumbling.

" Bataiye ..." Anubhav said.

" Pehle Durr toh hatiye..." Haseena said blushing.

" Nhi pehle bataiye...." Anubhav denied.

" Wo .. aa...aapke aur...hu... humare...b...baby ke ba... baare so...soch...rhi ...thi..." Haseena said blushing avoiding any eye contact with him.

" Aapka aur humara baby....ye kab hua..." Anubhav said without sensing the words she said.

Haseena quickly separated and got to her bed and covered her with quilt while Anubhav still revised her words.

" Pata nhi kiss buddhu insaan se pyaar Kiya hai...hum yaha bolne nervous horahe hai aur inhe ye abhi bhi nhi samajha...kya kare hum inka ...." Haseena murmured under her quilt.

" Kya ..behna yeh keh Rahi thi...." Anubhav finally realised the meaning.

" Ye kuch jyada nhi hogaya..." Anubhav said getting behind Haseena.

" Haseenaji ...ye aap blanket mein kyu chali gyi...kitni garmi hai ..." Anubhav said while Haseena face palmed herself.

" Hataiye ye..." Anubhav said pulling the blanket from her.

" Aap...itna kyu sharma rhi hai ..." Anubhav said cupping her face while Haseena avoided eye contact.

" Aise hi raha toh behna ki iccha kaise puri hogi..." Anubhav said adding more blush.

" Anubhav...." Haseena snuggled controlling her blush while Anubhav chuckled.

" Ek toh hume itna ajeeb lag raha tha ye batane mein aur upar se aapne samaj ne mein deri hogayi ..." Haseena complained.

" Acche se samaj gye hum unki dharnaaye...." Anubhav again teased.

" Chup hojaiye..." Haseena slightly beat his chest.

" Waise aapko itna ghabra na nhi chahiye tha jab hum aapke itne sameep aaye toh ..." Anubhav said caressing her hairs.

" Ek baat yaad rakhiye .... Hum aapko aapke izaazat ke bina kabhi kuch nhi karenge..." Anubhav said kissing her forehead.

" Thank you..." Haseena said contented.

Soon they drifted to a deep slumber after happy day.____________

Author's POV

A month more passed everyone were nearly healed and it became important to look after the case.

The remaining healing process would complete only after finding the culprits.____________

" Toh wakt aagaya hai humari manzil ki aur badhne ka " Anubhav said pouring all his heart.

" Toh shuruat karte hai...uss shoes se....kuch mila hai uss se...." Anubhav asked.

" Ji...kuch ret ke ansh mile hai....aur bomb making ke bhi..." Amar told what he got after the research.

" Ret ke nishaan...par usse hum bhi pohoch payenge anjam tak ..." Anubhav said

" Sir par bomb ke particles hai woh bohot high power ke hai ..." Amar said seriously.

" Matlab ye log kisi bomb factory mein hoke aaye the..." Cheetah said

" Par sir aise kitni factories hongi bomb manufacture karne waali... Hum kaise kisi ek ko dhundenge..." Santosh raised a question.

" Santosh...factories toh bohot hai ...par bohot kum aisi hai jaha pe ye gair kanuni dealing hoti ho ...." Anubhav answered.

" Hume ye jooto ke mahaan maalik ho dhundna hai pehle..." Anubhav said with a stern look.

" Par kaise Anu bhaiya....hum aapko bhaiya hi bolne Wale hai kuch maat bolana .." Karishma warned before he could speak while others smiled.

" Aasaan toh nhi hoga...par dhundana padega..." Anubhav said.

" Hume ek Suchi bannani hogi.. jisme unn sab ke naam honge joh humare Shak ke daire mein hai ..." Anubhav informed.

" Mere Shak ke daiyare mein wo dono brothers hi hai... devaliya brothers..." Shivani was clear about her suspicion.

" Ha wo aur uss village ka mantri..." Santosh added.

" Aap ek paper par likhti jaiye Santosh Sharma..." Anubhav ordered and Santosh followed.

" Ye mantri ka ho sakta hai .. unke paas powers bhi hai..." Binni said.

" Aur kaun ho sakta hai..." Anubhav asked.

" Rani..." Kareena spoke in unison and smiled at their telepathy.

" Rani...? " Anubhav asked.

" Wo nakli Qayamat...." Haseena answered.

" Hume lagta hai wo wapas aapna badala pura karne ke liye ye sab kar rhi ho..." Haseena said

" Ha ... already Hume dobaate dobaate pakadi gyi hai ..." Billu said.

" Likh lijiye naam..." Anubhav said to Santosh.

" Aur koi toh Aisa nhi hai...joh yeh sab karsakta ho...ya humse dushmani..." Pushpaji said.

" Pushpaji hum sab police wale hai...Hume khud ko nhi pata hota ki humare kitne dushman hai..." Anubhav spoke the fact.

" Woh toh hai ...." Pushpaji sadly said.

" Sir Mira ne joh locket laaya tha uska kya..." Santosh asked.

" Hum abhi laate hai..." Anubhav said getting up.

" Mira ...? Amma woh kahe aayi thi yaha..." Karishma said being frustrated.

" Woh Anubhav sir ne usse bheja tha...crime location pein saboot laane ke liye..." Santosh answered.

" Anu bhaiya bhi iss tinn ke dabbe ke changul mein fass gaye..." Karishma said irritated and Haseena sighed.

" Ye dekhiye ye locket hai wo..." Anubhav said bringing a complicatly designed triangle shape locket sealed in a bag.

" Bohot ajeeb hai iska sign..." Binni said looking at the locket.

" Pakka ye koi gang ka sign hoga..." Santosh said.

" Mein mobile pein scan karke dekhti hu..." Santosh said clicking a picture of locket.

" Kya hua kuch pata chala ..." Haseena asked.

" Nai ...ye Google bata rha hai ki ye samosa hai ..." Santosh said revealing the talent of the great image searcher while everyone laughed.

They continued their investigation for a long time .______________

" Aap kuch soch rhi hai..." Anubhav asked Haseena whose sleep was far away.

" Hume woh locket dekha dekha sa lag raha hai..." Haseena said thinking.

" Kaha .. " Anubhav asked.

" Wahi toh yaad nhi aaraha..." Haseena said closing her eyes and focusing.

" Accha abhi aap apne dimag par zor mat daaliye... sojaiyye...Apne AAP aajayega yaad..." Anubhav said tapping her forehead.

" Hmm ....." Haseena replied.

There's a little start to the mission!!

Who will be the mastermind behind this?

Where has Haseena seen the samosa locket?

To know keep reading" THE AFTERMATH "

Do vote & comment.

"Remember votes & comments, motivate me to write the next part early "

" Votes & Comments are key to early & interesting updates "

~ Kishaaa

First Move

Aaj sabka Dil tuta hai!Some of us knew this would happen phir bhi yaar sunke toh bura lagta na! Kitna bhi Mann bana liya ho everyone of us are sad more or less

101% nazar lagi hai humare show ko

Koi baat nhi hai as fans we have to support them in their further projects

____

Author's POV

The next day arrived signalling a new beginning.The patriots had already started planning their win yesterday.

Currently it was afternoon, sun shining bright giving whole summer vib es.Kids playing in their yards enjoying their vacation.

The Pawar Vada was all silent as all were busy discussing about the case._

____

" Aapko yaad aaya...? " Anubhav asked Haseena as they all gathered for their case discussion again.

" Nai...baar baar bas wo aankhon ke saamne aaraha hai...par pata nhi kaha dekha hai..." Haseena said still remembering.

" Par wo locket waha pein gir kaise Gaya..." Mihir questioned.

" Jija ji mujrim kitna bhi tez ho humesha koi saboot chod jata hai..." Anubhav answered.

" Filhaal Hume devalpar mein nazar rakhni hai...kyunki Shak ke daire mein sabse pehle wo hai.." Anubhav said

" Par nazar kaise rakhenge .." Amar asked.

" Waha pohoch kar..." Anubhav answered.

" Par bhaiya hum waha kaise jayenge...agar yaha se nikle toh sab kuch bahaar aajayega..." Karishma worried about the secrecy of the mission.

" Ha sir wo log hum sabko jaante hai..agar hum Gaye waha toh...humara bhanda phutt jayega ..." Pushpaji took worried.

" Ha agar Rani iske piche hogi toh woh aapko pehchaan legi..." Haseena added.

" Woh sab aapko jaante hai ..par mujhe toh nhi na..." Amar spoke.

" Bilkul sahi.. Devalpar ke log Amar ko nhi jaante...wahi waha jayega aur nazar rakhega..." Anubhav ordered.

" Akele...? Matlab...Binni ko bhi toh koi nhi jaanta...woh chali jayegi inke saath... ek se bhale do..." Shivani got scared for Amar for a second.

" Toh thik hai aap dono devalpar jayenge...waha ki stithi ko dekh ke hum aage kya karna hai sochenge..." Anubhav agreed while Binni too nodded positively.

" Kal subah aapko nikalna hai...Aur yaad rahe chehra jitna hosake itna chupa lena..." Anubhav asked them to be cautious.

" Ji hum dhyaan rakhenge..." Amar and Binni spoke.

Everyone got back to their rooms to rest for sometime.

" Cheete...tujhe kya lagta hai..kaun hosakta hai iske piche .." Santosh said leaning over Cheetah's shoulders.

" Hume kuch samajh nhi aaraha hai santuji... Pura humara dimaag Khali hogaya hai...jab bhi iske baare mein sochte hai na toh humara sir ghumne lagta hai..." Cheetah said sadly.

" Agar tujhe takleef hoti hai toh hum ye baat nhi karenge..." Santosh said.

" Hmm .." Cheetah agreed.

" Santuji hum na bohot khush hai ki aap humare saath hai...." Cheetah said looking at Santosh.

" Mai bhi....jab meri posting cyber mein thi na tab mai bohot akeli pad gyi thi ...na udhar tere , Pushpaji jaise colleagues the na Madam sir aur Karishma madam jaise seniors...sab bohot akdu the kaam se kaam rakhte the... koi hasta bhi nhi tha waha..." Santosh shared her experience.

" Wahi toh...humare mahila police Thane jaisi team kahi ho hi nhi sakti..." Cheetah spoke a fact.

" Hmm woh toh hai... isiliye mein udhar nhi jaane wali...mein yhi tum sabke saath kaam karungi...madam sir ko bhi mai mana lungi.." Santosh said

" Waise tune shaadi ke baare mein kya socha hai..." Santosh boldly asked.

" Shaadi...? Hum dono ki ..." Cheetah was surprised.

" Ha..tujhe nhi karni kya ... Ya mein dusra dhundu..." Santosh teased.

" Nai nai wo acchanak puch liya na aapne isiliye woh bohra Gaye hum.. .hum na aapko mission khatam hote hi humari Amma se milwayenge..." Cheetah said.

" Unhe mein pasand toh aaungi na...?" Santosh got tensed.

" Pasand...bohot jyada...Waise bhi humari Amma rah dekh rhi hai ki kab hum unhe unki bahu se milwayenge..." Cheetah smilingly said.

" Unhe mere baare mein pata hai...?" Santosh surprisingly asked.

" Ha ..hum humari maa se sab kuch batiyate hai..." Cheetah confidently said.

" Par ek problem hai...Tujhe mere bhai aur papa ko manana hoga..." Santosh said sadly.

" Hum karlenge wo..." Cheetah said holding Santosh tightly.

" Agar meri mummy hoti na toh...wo mana leti unhe... par pata nhi kyu wo mujhe itni jaldi kyu chod chale gyi..." Santosh teared up.

" Santuji aapko pata hai na ki hume aapke aankhon mein aansu bilkul acche nhi lagte .. Aur jab aap humari Amma se milengi na toh aapko bohot accha Lage ga..wo aapko unki beti bana ke rakhengi..." Cheetah said wiping her tears.

" Thank you cheete..." Santosh said putting her head on his chest.

Cheetah kissed her cheek instantly and Santosh looked up blushing.Yes it was the first kiss!

" Aap toh sharma gyi santu ji .." Cheetah said smiling.

Santosh quickly hide her face and both dozed off to sleep.

(Tbh.. Cheetosh romance likhna bahut hard hai!! No offense)

" Thodi der aaram karlo karu kabse jagi Hui ho .." Mihir said to Karishma.

" Patidev..." Karishma hugged Mihir.

" Bolo.." Mihir asked her to speak.

" Humare baby jaha bhi hoga khush hoga na..." Karishma dreamly spoke.

" Woh jaha bhi hoga khush hoga... Aur humne kaha na ki uss baare mat socho...thik nhi hai tumhare liye .." Mihir said caressing her hairs.

" Hmm ..nhi sochenge...". Karishma agreed.

" Aaram Karo thodi der..." Mihir said tapping her forehead.

" Ammaa kaun hai khat khat kar raha hai... patidev de khiye na ..." Karishma chided as her good 2hr sleep broke.

" Ye kaha chale gye...lagta bahar honge .." Karishma said finding the bed empty.

" Par ye khat khat kaun kar raha hai " Karishma looked here and there.

" Shuk...shuk..." A voice was heard.

" Kaun hai waha..." Karishma said looking towards window from where the sound came but nobody was seen.

" Kaun hai..." Karishma again said being alert.

The patriots are ready for their first step!!

I tried writing a bit of Cheetosh but it's hard for me!!Hope you are happy with the bit of Cheetosh I wrote!!

What do you think..? Who's at the window?

To know keep reading" THE AFTERMATH "

Do vote & comment.

"Remember votes & comments, motivate me to write the next part early "

" Votes & Comments are key to early & interesting updates "

~ Kishaaa

Enigmatic

" **K**aun hai waha..." Karishma said looking towards window from where the sound came but nobody was seen.

" Kaun hai..." Karishma again said being alert.

Taking the bottle kept on the table Karishma moved towards the window.

She was about to hit the person but the person screamed.

" Aaaaa..." The person screamed closing eyes and was about to fall off.

" Aree ...." Karishma says holding the person's hand and saving.

Illustration:-

(Meri drawing pein na jao...wo Google baba ne acchi photo nhi dikhayi isiliye mujhe kalakari dikhani padi hadbadi mein...waise I am very good at drawing)

" Tum kaun ho...tum gir kese rhi thi..." Karishma said as the girl balanced herself again.

" Tumhari vajah se...ek toh meri height choti aur tum aayi baatli leke maarne aayi mujhe...Mera pair fisal Gaya iss dagad se..." The girl said in a maharashtrian accent messing up the whole language.

" Par kar kya Rahi ho...aur humare kamre mein kyu jhaak rhi ho .." Karishma asked.

" Tum kyu phaltu ke sawaal puch rhi hai...mujhe meri kairi wapas do ..." The girl said peeping in the room.

" Kairi ..? " Karishma asked confused.

" Ha kairi...Maine itni garmi mein ped par chadkar todi hai ... Wo idhar kholi mei aake gir gyi...kaha hai khayi toh nhi na tumne.." The little girl said peeping in again.

" Itti si toh hai...lekin baate kaise kar rhi ho..." Karishma said looking at the girl.

" Itti si nhi hu...pure 8 saal ki hu...Pehle tum mujhe kairi doh meri ...mujhe jaana hai...kisine dekh liya toh poblem hojayegi..." The little said in a irritated tone.

" Problem hota hai wo poblen nhi...Kaha hai..." Karishma began looking for the Kairi.

" Ye lo..." Karishma gave her the fruit.

" Dhanyawad... mujhe jaana hoga..." The girl said and was to climb down the stone when Karishma stopped her.

" Aree ruko...naam kya hai tumhara..." Karishma asked.

" Mai kisi anjaan ko naam nhi batati...chalo mujhe jaane doh... Shivani dekhlengi toh poblem hojayegi...." The girl said and was about to go but Karishma again holded her hand.

" Ruko...ye chot kaise aayi tumhe..." Karishma asked seeing her hand full of scratches.

" Aree ye...mamuli chot hai...roz lagti hai...ped pein chadke...thik hojaye gi..." The girl said dramatically.

" Ruko..." Karishma asked her to stop.

" Aree par ..." The girl was about to deny but Karishma interrupted.

" Humne kaha na ruko ..." Karishma said glaring.

Karishma grabbed the first aid box and approached towards the girl.

" Haath aage Karo..." Karishma ordered but the girl just looked at her.

" Sunayi nhi deta kya..." Karishma said taking her hand front.

" Aah ..kya kar rhi ho ..." The girl winced in pain.

" Dawai laga rahe hai... agar thode din aise hi chod deti chot ko toh...sach mein poblem hojati " Karishma said applying the ointment.

" Aap khud poblem bolo chalega par mai bolu toh meri galti nikaloge..." The girl said keeping her one hand on her waist in bossy manner.

" Kyunki tum choti ho...galti sudharni chahiye tumhe...aur ye parivartan kaise abhi toh jhagad rhi thi...tu tu mai mai karke aur abhi achanak se aap..." Karishma said looking towards her.

" Ha ... kyunki aap pehli ho... jisne mujhe meri chot ke baare pucha...aur dawai bhi lagayi...isse pehle kisine ye nhi pucha ..." The girl said looking at Karishma with her red eyes.

" Ek min..." Karishma again tried to stop her.

" Nhi ..abhi nhi...mujhe jaana hai.. phir milenge..." The girl said smiling.

" Phir milenge kyu .." Karishma questioned

" Kyunki mujhe lagta hai...aur mujhe joh lagta hai wo sach hota hai..." The girl simply said.

" Aur ha Shivani ko ye matt batana ki mai yaha aayi thi...nai toh mujhe kaccha jaba jayegi wo...Aur ye aapki chot bhi jaldi se thik hojaye.." The girl said touching her little hands on Karishma's forehead caressing the wound and ran from there.

" Ajeeb ladki hai ..bhala Shivani isse kahe kaccha chaba jayegi... Aur kehti hai phir milenge .. chakri hai ekdam ...par bohot pyaari hai .." Karishma said thinking about her.

" Kya re...akele kyu muskura rhi hai...aur Maine bola na ki khidki band rakh... kisine dekhliya toh problem hojayegi ..." Shivani said closing the windows.

" Ha wo garmi bohot thi... isiliye kholi thi..." Karishma said coming out of the world.

" Chal bahar...sab bula rahe .." Shivani said

" Ha chalo..." Karishma said and went with her.____________

" Toh ye rhi aapki train ki ticket aapko subah 6 baje nikalna hai..." Anubhav said forwarding two tickets to Amar.

" Hume waha ki har ek sukshma khabar chahiye...." Anubhav said to Amar and Binni.

" Kya bola aapne ..suk..shma...?" Santosh asked confusedly.

" Choti choti khabar santu..." Pushpaji explained her.

" Ohh...! " Santosh understood.

" Baaki aapko sab kuch samajha diya gya hai..." Anubhav said.

" Ji...." Amar and Binni nodded.___________

Author's POV

The moon took his place in the sky bringing peaceful night.Santosh was helping Binni pack her bag for the mission.Their friendship was blooming each passing day._______________

" Nervous toh nhi ho..." Santosh asked.

" Nai... nervous kyu ho ungi Mai...ulta accha lag raha ki tum police walo ki madat kar rhi hu..." Binni said with a smile.

" Chalo accha hai..." Santosh too smiled.______________

Author's POV

Amar was busy packing his own luggage to be taken to the mission when Shivani entered.Starling him Shivani hugged him from back.___________
___

" Kya baat hai...Aaj Chand kaha se nikla hai..." Amar said smiling.

" Aisa kyu bol rhe ho..." Shivani asked still being in the same position.

" Aise aaj pehli baar itne dino mein tumne mujhe hug kiya hai.. " Amar said turning towards her.

" Ha tum toh kal jaa rahe ho na..." Shivani said being emotional.

" Aree baby ...tum kabse senti hone lagi...Mai thode din mein wapas aajauga ...." Amar said cupping her face.

" Phir bhi Darr toh Lage na..." Shivani said keeping her head on his chest.

" Chinta matt Karo jaldi aur sahi salamat aaunga...Aur wo tumhari gundi behen haina... uske hote hue kya chinta..." Amar said caressing her hairs.

" Tumpe dhyaan rakhne ke liye hi bheja hai...aur gundi mat bolo behen hai wo meri...aur tumhari hone wali saali..." Shivani said looking at him.

" Accha itni jaldi hai shaadi ki ..." Amar said teasing while Shivani hid her face in his chest.

Amar cupped her face and kissed her forehead and Shivani smiled in peace.

" Amar ye rahe camera aur mikes..." Anubhav entered but thanks to camera and mikes he was busy looking at them Shivani quickly separated from Amar and maintained a distance.

" Aap yaha...?" Anubhav asked.

" Ha...woh ye ... charge me Dene aayi thi..." Amar answered fumbling.

" Accha ..." Anubhav suspiciously agreed.

" Mai chalti hu....binni se bhi milna hai... Amar sir best of luck mission ke liye ..." Shivani quickly left.

" Kya baat hai Amar...kuch chupa rahe ho..? " Anubhav asked.

" Nai ..wo bas thoda mission ko leke nervous hu .." Amar lied.

" Chinta matt Karo sab thik hoga..." Anubhav calmed him believing in his lie for now.

The part came up with the new lovers moments#ShivaniAmar

The mystery person's mystery is a little unveiled!!!

Who's the person? Whats her role here?

To know keep reading" THE AFTERMATH "

Do vote & comment.

"Remember votes & comments, motivate me to write the next part early "

" Votes & Comments are key to early & interesting updates "

~ Kishaaa

Commencing

<hr>

The weather outside was a little cold and pleasant. It was the day today when Amar and Binni were leaving for Devalpar. The train was sharp at 6 in the morning. Hence the whole Pawar Vada had woken up before the sunrise. ________

" Best of luck aap dono ko..." Haseena wished for the mission.

" Acche se sambhal lena...pal pal ki khabre dete rahiye... " Anubhav said.

" Ha... Khaas kar use mantri par dhyaan dena Amar sir... " Santosh said.

" Ji... Aap chinta Matt kijiye hum dono sab sambhalenge.. " Amar said smilingly.

" Ye lijiye dahi shakhar khaa lijiye... " Pushpaji said feeding both of them.

Avoiding any vehile sound in the morning Amar, Binni, Anubhav, Mihir and Shivani decided to leave for the station walking...

Amar went out with his luggage and Shivani followed him.

" Dhyaan rakhna aapna... " Shivani said with teary eyes.

" Tim bhi... aur aakhon se aansu bilkul Matt nikalna..."Amar said wiping her tears.

"Hmmm.. " Shivani hugged him but quickly separate realising they were outside the house unfortunately unknown to the couple someone saw the scene.

" Chaliye nikalte hai.... " Mihir said coming with Binni and Anubhav.

" Binni acche se rehna... aur gusse par kabu rakhna..."Shivani said as they started walking.

" Chinta na kar tu Jiji.... manne pata hai... sab sambhal lungi... " Binni said putting her hands over Shivani's shoulder.

" Aap aise samajha rhi hai jaise aap humari behna ko samjha rhi hai... " Anubhav said smiling.

" Ha toh ye usse kam thodi... Do do daroga hai humare team mein... " Shivani said while everyone chuckled.

The trio left them outside the station and started their walk way back to the Vada.

Author's POV

Haseena, Puspaji and Cheetosh were the ones who were awake but again went to their rooms to take fresh quick nap.

Nobody waked Karishma up considering her health. _____________

" Tak tak... " A knock was heard.

" Amaa.. phirse.. awaaz aane lagi.. subah se chaar baar aap chuki hai... " Karishma chided as her sleep got disturbed.

" Lagta hai woh chuhiya hogi...par ab kahe...ab toh uska aam bhi nhi gira yaha... " Karishma said getting up.

" Shivani ne mana kiya hai khidki kholne se..." Karishma thought before opening the window.

" Subah subah kaun dekhe ga...khol hi lete hai..." Karishma openef the window.

" Kitni der mai kabse khat khat kar rhi hu..." The little girl chided.

" Hum so rahe the...tum itni subah yaha kya kar rhi ho...aur ye kya hai tumhare haath mein..." Karishma said looking at her.

" Yahi dene aayi thi mein...yaha ke bappa ka prashaad...bohot chamatkari hai...khakar dekhna tumhari chote aapne aap thik hojayegi..." The girl said forwading the paper bowl to Karishma.

" Tumhe koi daant ta nhi...itni subah yaha aagayi..kal bhi kitna andhera tha yaha..." Karishma said out of concern to which the little girl's face fell

" Koi daant ne wala nhi hai...yhi anaath asharam mein rehti hu..." The girl said strongly but controlling her tears.

" Mujhe maaf karna..." Karishma said carressing her face lovingly.

" Prasad kha lena...Tum mujhe acchi lagi isiliye pehli baar kisi ke liye laayi hu..." The girl said with heavy voice.

" Pehle tum khalo..." Karishma said feeding her.

" Mai chalti hu...Shivani dekh legi..." The girl said avoiding eye contact with Karishma and left.

" Bechari...hum bhi topa hai..aisa nhi puchna chahiye tha usse...bohot bura laga hoga usse..." Karishma said closing the window.

Karishma freshened up and firstly ate the prasaad not before taking god's name.

" Uss..bacchi ko humesha khush rakhna..." Karishma prayed.___________

—

Author' POV

The skies turned in the tint of pink as the sun sinked.The people of Chako-rgao were as usual busy buying vegetables like every evening.___________

" Hello...Kaisi hai tu..." The little girl met Shivani the same day evening.

" Mai thik hi hu...tu phir se yaha waha ghumne lagi.." Shivani said while paying the vendor.

" Ha...toh waha mein kya karu...yaha bahar ghumi toh kisi baat toh kar sakti hu..." The girl said while walking with Shivani to the next vendor.

" Waise mujhe kuch pata chal gaya hai..." The little girl said looking at Shivani.

" Kya pata chala hai...aur mujhe aise kyu dekh rhi hai..." Shivani questioned.

" Yaha nhi...tu sabzi kharid le phir mein bataungi..." The girl said.

" Mere paas wakt nhi hai...ghar par mehmaan hai...bol jaldi..." Shivani said putting a bunch of spinach in her bag.

" Tera chakkar chal rha haina..." The girl said in excitement.

" Ae kya bol rhi hai...dhire bol..." Shivani said closing her mouth.

" Maine pehle hi kaha tha...khi aur chal par tu gi nhi maani..." The girl said.

" Accha chal..." Shivani took her far away from crowd.

" Maine subha tumhe aut uss lambeee pole ko dekha tha... " The girl said actioning her words.

" Kya lambe pole..." Shivani asked confusedly.

" Ha...tu ro rhi thi aur wo tere aansu poch raha tha...Phir usne tujhe gale bhi laga liya..." The girl said teasingly.

" Tu waha kya kar rhi thi...itni subah..." Shivani asked bending to her height.

" Mai toh mandir se laut rhi thi...." The girl said casually.

" Thik hai..tujhe pata chal gaya hai toh...kisi ko batana mattt.." Shivani said.

" Aree aise kaise na batau...mai toh ye taaza khabar pure Chakorgao mein bolungi..." The little girl said with attitude.

" Accha thik hai...tu bolde...phir mein tujhe mere ped se kairiya nhi lene dungi.." Shivani tried to bribe her.

" Yahi toh sunna tha mujhe...mai kisi ko nhi bata ungi...par mujhe kairi todne nhi rokegi..." The girl said with a smirk.

" Accha thik hai...par kisi ko matt batana..." Shivani accepted her defeat.

" Tujhi shapat..." The girl said pinching her throat signalling a promise.

" Ab sidhe aashram jaana yaha waha mat bhatakna..." Shivani said ruffling the girl's hair smiling.

" Tata...." The waved Shivani and left.-

On reaching Devalpar what will Amar and Binni find?

Will they get proofs that they're looking for?

What's the mystery of the little girl?

How is she so friendly with Shivani?

To know keep reading" THE AFTERMATH "

Do vote & comment.

"Remember votes & comments, motivate me to write the next part early "

" Votes & Comments are key to early & interesting updates "

~ Kishaaa

Devalpar

A uthor's POV

Amar dressed in a yellow tshirt and paired with a blue denim,the attractive sunglasses adding 5 stars in his outfit while Binni dressed in a dyed jumpsuit with sneakers,hair tied in a high ponytail with sunglasses giving her a wow look reached Devalpar.The sight here was unusual.The always silent village with a pressure of punishment was now a happily living village.Amar and Binni were confused about what MPT members told them.Surprisingly no one stopped them at the entry as Haseena and Karishma were stopped before getting in.Amar and Binni got a smooth entry in the village.

On entering they were shocked to see little girls playing carefree but as told by Haseena,people here were brainwashed by the Devaliya brothers in case of a girl child._____________

" Eee...toh chamatkaar hai..." Binni said looking around.

" Ha...jaisa bataya waisa kuch nhi hai..." Amar too said looking around.

" Bacchiya bhi kitni shaanti se khel rahi..." Binni said looking at the girls.

" Aree...aap seher se aaye hai ka.? " A elderly man approached both of them.

" Ji...Wo humara survey hai yaha..." Amar faked his job.

" Rukiye...rukiye 5 minat.." The elderly man asked him to stop.

Both squinted there eyes expecting something weird or wrong but they again lost.

" Humara niyam hai...kisi bhi baahar ke logo ko aarti utare bina andar nhi jane de sakte..." A elderly woman said coming with a plate of Aarti.

" Ha aakhir mehmaan bhagwaan ka roop hota hai..." The elderly man supported his wife.

" Aap pati patni hai ka...?" The elderly woman asked once her Aarti was finished.

" Nhi...nhi...ye behen hai humari...patni..nhi.." Amar cleared the misunderstanding quickly.

" Ha behen hai hum inki.." Binni got added.

" Accha accha...maaf kijiye ye Susheela kuch bhi...puchti rehti hai..." The elderly man apologized.

"Aaiye...hum aapko kamra dikha dete hai..." The elderly man took him to a cottage.

" Yeh hai aapka kamra...do wakt ka khana aur chai yaha aa jayega...aap aaram se apna kaam kar sakte hai..." The elderly man said smilingly.

" Thank you...waise aap yaha ke sarpanch...?" Amar asked.

" Nhi...nhi hum itne bade kaha...wo kya hai na humare gao mein koi bhi sarpanch ya phir hukum chalane wala nhi hai...wo bas harr roz yaha ke harr jodi ye kaam sambhalti hai..." The elderly man politely explained.

" Aisa kahe...Gao hai...sarpanch kaise nhi..." Binni asked.

" Wo ka hai na...ki humare gao ke do bhai the...bohot julm karte the hum sab par...par ek baar ek bacchi ne awaaz uthaya aur bhagwaan ki kripa se police walo ne unhe sabak sikha diya...isiliye abhi sab khush hai yaha...." The man told the history.

" Woh dono bhai kaha hai ab..." Amar asked.

" Unn kamino ko unki manzil mil gyi..." The man said.

" Matlab...?" Binni asked

" Kisi baalik ladki par atyachaar kiya unn dono bhaiyo ne aur kisi paksh ke mantri ne...isiliye unhe saza de di...par unn tino ne aatmahatya karli..." The man explained.

" Accha..." Binni said.

" Hum chalte hai...bohot kaam hai hume..." The man said and left.

Amar closed the door and both sat on the bed.

" Yaha toh sab badal gaya hai..." Amar said thinking.

" Matlab ye tino toh nhi hosakte gunhegaar...." Binni added.

" Hum Anubhav ko call karte hai..." Amar said taking his phone out.

" Aree rukiye hum pehle ye sab kapde badal lein....kaise kapde diye jiji ne..." Binni irritatedly said as sge found those clothes uncomfortable.

" Ji...mai rukta hu..." Amar said chuckling

Binni quickly went off to washroom.

" Thik ho..." Amar said on a call with Shivani.

" Mai thik hi hu...par tumne phone kyu kiya...binni ko pata chala na toh woh puri duniya ko bata degi..." Shivani answered.

" Aree wo kapde badal rhi hai...5 minute pehle tumhe hi gaaliya de rhi thi...". Amar said.

" Kya...mujhe gaaliya de rhi thi..." Shivani asked.

" ha...tumne jo usse kapde diye na...wo usse pasand nhi aaye isiliye..." Amar said chuckling.

" Pagal hai wo..." Shivani said.

" Accha chalo mai rakhta hu..." Amar said.

" I love you..." Shivani replied.

" I love you too..." Amar said back.

" I love you...? " Binni said coming out.

(Bgm..Lagi lagi lag gyi...)

" Kisse baat kar rahe hai aap..." Binni said getting to him.

" Wo Shivani se..." Amar was about to spit the truth.

" Kya...aap jiji ko i love you bol rahe tha...? " Binni said shockingly while Shivani facepalmed her self on the other side.

" Nai...mai bunty se mere bete se baat kar raha tha..." Amar concealed.

" Toh jiji ka naam kaise aaya..." Binni said squinting her eyes.

" Aree wo bunty ne call kaat diya...Shivani waiting par thi..." Amar faked.

" Sachmein...." Binni said.

" Baat nhi karni unse..." Amar asked in sarcastic way.

" Aree jiji...kaise kapde diye the tune..." Binni started complaining snatching phone from Amar.

" Tu pehle mission ke baare bata...sab sun rahe hai tujhe..." Shivani said looking at everyone.

" Ha...sorry.." Binni got embrassed.

" Kya haal hai waha ka Amar..." Anubhav asked.

" Puchiye matt...aapke hosh udd jayenge sunn ke.." Amar said

" Maine kaha na..wahi log criminal hai..." Santosh quickly came to conclusion.

" Nhi...santosh...tu yaha jisse criminal bol rhi thi...unka toh kab ka the end ho chuka hai..." Binni said shocking everybody.

" Aayein.." Santosh quintupleted.

" Khul ke bataiye..." Karishma roared.

Amar & Binni narrated the whole incident.

" Matlab inpe shak karke koi fayda nhi..." Anubhav concluded.

" Aap kal hi phir aajaiye...aage ka plan bhi sochna hoga..." Anubhav said.

" Ji..." Amar and Binni agreed.

" Rakhte hai phone..." Anubhav said and disconnected.

" Ab toh humare shak ke dairee mein sirf Rani hi bachi hai..." Haseena said.

" Par uss tak pohochenge kaise..." Cheetah asked.

" Sochne ke liye wakt chahiye hume...jaldbaazi nhi kar sakte...Amar aur Binni ko aane dijiye phir aage ka sochenge..." Anubhav said.

" Aap sab bhi aapne dimaag par jor matt daliye...health ke liye thik nhi hai..." Mihir said.

" Aaram kijiye aap log..." Anubhav said.

Devaliya brothers & Mantriji are out of box now!!

If not Devaliya brothers then whose behind all this?

How will the team investigate upon Rani?

To know keep reading" THE AFTERMATH "

Do vote & comment.

"Remember votes & comments, motivate me to write the next part early "

" Votes & Comments are key to early & interesting updates "

~ Kishaaa

Enthusiastic

Author's POV

Amar and Binni had returned the next day finding no clue about the bomb blast.The team now had to think of a new plan regarding the new suspicions.________

" Humne kuch socha hai..." Anubhav said.

" Kaash mein aapke dimaag mein ghus ke aapne jo socha hai wo sun sakti..." Santosh said out of innocence while other glared at her.

" Toh humara agla shak Rani yani Qayamat ke upar jaata hai..." Anubhav continued.

" Amma...humare taraf kyu dekh rhe ho sab..." Karishma yelled seeing MPT members gazes towards her.

" Wahi toh...Anubhav sir...Sirf Qayamat nhi...Nakli qayamat..kyunk i orginal wali toh humari Karishma madam hai..." Santosh innocence again rose.

" Amma jadbuddhi....kuch bhi bole jaa rhi...shaunk hai ka humse pitne ka...ya yaha singhade nhi milte..." Karishma scolded.

" Sahi toh keh rahi thi bechari..." Pushpaji murmured but Karishma heard.

" Aa...chup...hume mission pein dhyaan dena hai..." Haseena ceased the war before Karishma could answer Pushpaji.

" Anu...humare matlab hai Anubhav sir continue" Haseena said looking at Anubhav correcting her mistake.

" Toh...nakli qayamat...hai humara agla shak..." Anubhav continued looking at Santosh.

" Aur jiske baare mein humen koi aata pata nhi hai..." Anubhav said.

" Last time wo...Naina ke case ke liye arrest hui thi..." Haseena said.

" Kitne wakt pehle...?" Anubhav asked.

" Yhi kuch 4-5 mahine pehle..." Haseena answered.

" Ho sakta haina bhaiya ki wo wapas badala lene ke liye kar rhi ho..." Karishma said.

" Ha...waise bhi wo teen baar kar chuki hai ye..." Cheetah added.

" Par agar aap uske whereabouts nhi jaante toh nai jante toh kaise pata lagayenge uske baare mein..." Amar asked the right question.

" Humare paas ek plan hai...Jisse agar Rani criminal hai toh woh bhi pakdi jayegi ya phir agar koi aur criminal ho...wo bhi pakada jayega..." Anubhav said in determined tone.

" Kya plan hai..." Everyone said together making Anubhav smile at their dedication.

" Hum lucknow jayenge...phir headquarters se khabar prakashit karenge ...ki MPT ka case reopen ho chuka hai..aur uski investigation IB karegi..." Anubhav narrated his plan.

" Usse kya hoga..." Binni asked.

" Ye baat uss criminal tak toh jarur pohochengi...phir wo hume rokne ke liye...kuch toh saazish karenge hi na..." Anubhav said with a smirk.

" Lekin iss mein aap ki jaan ki bohot khatra hai Anubhav" Haseena got scared.

" Aap toh jaanti hai hum humare desh ke liye kuch bhi kar sakte hai...Hume kuch nhi hoga..." Anubhav said in determined tone.

" Lekin bhaiya wo criminal bohot khatarnaak ho sakta hai...kuch bhi kar ega.." His little sister got scared this time.

" Aap toh hume bachpan se jaanti hai behna aap toh aisa matt kahiye..." Anubhav smiled at Karishma.

" Toh hum kal lucknow ke liye niklenge...Aur tab tak wapas nhi aayenge jab tak unn gunhegaaro ko nhi pakad lete..." Anubhav declared.

" Wo...sir mai bhi chalu aapke saath...?" Santosh asked.

" Hum kaafi hai... " Anubhav didn't want to risk his new sister's life.

" Par sir ek se bhale do ho jayenge...waise bhi mujhe bhi badala lena hai unse..." Santosh tried to convince him.

" Thik hai..." Anubhav finally agreed after lot of convincing.__________

————

Author's POV

Haseena was helping Anubhav packing his bag controlling her emotions. She had finally got her love back after a long war she didn't want him to risk his life again.But the weakest point in their life was " Desh ke liye kuch bhi " .The amount of love and respect the couple had for their country was the thing that made them risk their life again and again.And here,the subject was not only country but also the revenge of hurting Anubhav's loved one's.Then on who's saying would Anubhav step back!!No ones!!!Hence Haseena stayed quiet.___________

" Ye blanket bhi rakh lijiye...kya pata achanak thandi pad jaye waha..." Haseena said keeping a blanket in the suitcase.

Anubhav moved towards Haseena who was avoiding eye contact since the discussion.Holding her chin,Anubhav lifted her face only to find her eyes teary.

" Aap jaanti hai na..aapke ye aansu...hume acche nhi lagte..." Anubhav said looking into Haseena's eyes.

" Isiliye toh kuch nhi bol rahe...kyunki hum aapko kamzor karke mission pein bhejna nhi chahte hai...Hum jaante hai desh aapke liye sabse pehle ha i...aur yaha baat toh aapke parivaar ki bhi hai...kaise rukenge aap.." Haseena expressed.

" Hum jaante hai...aap jarur uss criminal tak pohochenge...Aur wapas shi salamat aayenge..." Haseena said taking his hand into hers.

" Wapas kaise na aaye...itni khubsurat wajah hai humare paas..." Anubhav said pecking Haseena's palm.

" Aur humari Santu ka dhyaan rakhna...pehli baar itni high profile case par jara rhi hai.." Haseena got concerned about her sister.

" Jaante hai...par aap unhe apni behen matt banaiye...kyunki phir hum bhi aapke bhai ban jayenge...aur hume ye manzoor nhi hai..." Anubhav said to lighten Haseena's mood.

" Kuch bhi..." Haseena chuckled and hugged him.

" Aandar aaye hum..." Karishma and Mihir at the door.

" Ye lijiye bhaiyaa...humari taraf se aapka lucky charm.." Karishma said handling a tiffin to him.

" Aisa kya lucky charm hai joh tiffin mein aata ho..." Haseena questioned.

" Desi ghee ke ladu.." Anubhav said sensing the aroma.

" Humare banaye hue laddo bhaiya ke liye humesha lucky hote hai..." Karishma said.

" Ab toh hum criminals tak pohoch hi jayenge..." Anubhav said smiling.

" Khyaal rakhiye aapna..." Karishma and Mihir said as Anubhav took them in a hug.

" Humari taraf se bhi kuch hai..." Pushpaji said coming in.

" Ye kaal dhaaga...humesha aapki raksha karega..." Pushpaji said tying a thread along Anubhav's wrist while Anubhav touched her feet.

" Sir....mujhe mera billu niwas aur aap dono chahiye..." Billu said.

" Bilkul shreeman..." Anubhav said.

" Ha sir aur aap aapka aur humari santuji ka khyaal rakhna..." Cheetah said.

" Jarur..." Anubhav said

And they shared a hug.

" Hume bhi lo...hum bhi toh hissa hai ab..." Shivani said standing at the door with Amar and Binni.

" Ek min...Santu kaha hai..." Haseena said at absense of Santosh.

" Yaha hu mein..." Santosh said standing at the door.

" Ye kya lagaya hai aapne..." Haseena asked.

" Facepack madam sir...mission hai kal presentable toh lagna chahiye.."A carefree Santosh said instead of getting tensed about the mission.

"Aap soch rahe honge...mai itni chill kaise hu...aree jab mere saath itne hatte katte Anu bhaiya hai...toh mai bhala tension lu.." Santosh said making everybody laugh and joined the hug.

Anubhav found a way towards there goal!!

It might be risky but "Desh ke liye kuch bhi" is on!!!

Indeed its everyone's enthusiasm that's helping them reach there goal..

How will Santosh and Anubhav cope with the hurdles in their way?

To know keep reading" THE AFTERMATH "

Do vote & comment.

"Remember votes & comments, motivate me to write the next part early "

" Votes & Comments are key to early & interesting updates "

~ Kishaaa

Lucknow

- -

Author's POV

Anubhav and Santosh were all ready to return to their city.Everyone were scared about there lives but decided to be quite as this might loosen there confidence.__________

" Santu rakh liya na sab..." Pushpaji asked for the nth time.

" Rakh liya pushpaji...cheetah bhi subah se 10 baar puch chuka hai..." Santosh said irritated.

" Mujhe school picnic wali feeling aarahi hai...mai koi choti bacchi hu joh aap sab mujhe baar sab puch rahe hai..." Santosh chided.

" Tum choti hi ho jyaada uddo matt..." Pushpaji scolded her like a mother.

" Pushpee naraz ho gyi aap toh..." Santosh said hugging Pushpaji.

" Ha..toh...tujhe maine kabhi apni beti se kam mana hai kya..." Pushpaji said teary.

" Aree aap ro mat na Pushpaji..." Santosh said being in the hug.

" Nhi ro rahe...bas aap dono khyaal rakhiye apna..." Pushpaji said.

" Maine pehle bhi kaha tha...ye hatte katte anu bhaiya hai na...kuch nhi hone denge..." Santosh said looking at Anubhav.

" Ha hum inhe kuch nhi hone denge..." Anubhav said taking Santosh in a side hug.

" Chaliye ab nikalte hai..." Anubhav said.

" Anubhav..." Haseena hugged him tightly closing her eyes while Anubhav kissed her forehead irrespective of everyone's presence.

Haseena soon separated and Karishma hugged her brother.

" Aap sab bhi aapna khyaal rakhiye...Dawaiyya samai se liya kariye..." Anubhav advised.

" Hmm..." Everyone replied.__________

Author's POV

Around 2 in the noon Santosh and Anubhav reached Lucknow.As Anubhav had already informed in headquarters about their arrival a special cab with police protection was sent to pick them.Anubhav didn't provide any details neither about the train nor from where did the duo departed for security purposes.The police cab directly took them to headquarters.___

____

" Jai hind sir..." Anubhav and Santosh saluted the commissioner of Lucknow

" Mai khush hu ki koi toh saamne aaya iss case ko reopen karne ke liye..." The senior said proudly.

" Kaise nhi aate...Mahila Police Thana humara pariwaar reh chuka hai..." Anubhav emotionally said.

" Janta hu..." The commissioner being Anubhav's bestfriend understood his feelings and patted his shoulders.

" Aap bhi reh chuki hai na MPT ki member..." The commissioner asked Santosh.

" Ha...cyber cell ke transfer se pehle MPT mein hi posted thi..." Santosh said maturely.

" Toh jaise ki aap dono iss case se emotionally attached hai...toh aapko iss case ke chalte aapke jazbaaton case pein havi nhi hone dena hai..." The senior seriously said.

"Ji sir..." Anubhav and Santosh confidently replied.

" Toh aap chahe toh abhi investigation shuru kar sakte hai...aur plan ke hisaab se media mein bhi ye news viral hojayegi..." The commissioner said while the duo nodded.

" Toh hum nikalte hai...." Anubhav said and both left.____________

Author's POV

A car with police badge stopped on the road of Mahila Police Thana.As Santosh & Anubhav stepped out of the car all the sweet memories flashed in front of their eyes making them weak for a sec.A huge photo frame of our near and dear police officers who lost their lives in the blast was kept in the centre supported by a small pot of a baby tree planted by the MPT probably placed byIqbal & Badnaam.

The aroma of delicious biryani and tea catched their attention next.Both looked towards the shop of the dear vendors.Anubhav and Santosh entered their stall.Anubhav banged his fingers on the table and ordered tea just like a customer.

Badnaam turned only find two known persons.Iqbal too turned and was shocked seeing the duo._____________

" Zeher nhi pilaoge Badnaam..." Santosh said with a smile.

" Aap yaha...? " Badnaam questioned still processing the happening.

" Jarur aap dono iss kaand ke piche ke gunhegaaro ko pakadne aaye ho..." Iqbal emotionally said.

" Ji haa....ab wo dinn durr nhi jiss din hum un logo saza denge..." Anubhav said.

" Sir...humare pyaare dost toh wapas nhi aayenge na...unhe toh maar diya unhone..." Iqbal said remembering the MPT members.

" Par unhe nyaay dena humara kartvya hai na...toh hum woh toh kar hi sakte hai..." Anubhav said.

" Baithiye na aap dono....kitne din hogaye zeher nhi pilaya kisi ko..." Badnaam asked them to have a sit.

Anubhav and Santosh sat reminiscing the old memories.While having a talk Santosh noticed a suspicious man at Iqbal's hair salon probably keeping an eye on them through the mirror.Santosh immediately alerted Anubhav who thought to look after it in few minutes giving no idea to the person.

" Lagta hai aapka dhanda bad gaya...Aapne bhi dukaan pein naukar laga diye..." Anubhav said to Iqbal.

" Ha...3 mahine pehle hi jude hai ye...unhe bhi kaam ki jarurat thi aur humara bhi kaam halka hogaya..." Iqbal answered.

" Accha hai..." Anubhav sighed.

Santosh and Anubhav headed towards the crime location which was sealed with red ribbon from all the four side. Anubhav unlocked the seal and both entered and started looking for proofs.

" Hume chalna chahiye...jitni aag lagani thi laga chuke hai...aur isme koi shak nhi hai ki wo ussi shaks ka aadmi hai jinhone yeh sab kiya hai..." Anubhav secretly said this to Santosh.

" Ji sirr..." Santosh replied and soon they headed towards a house arranged by the force.___________

" Kya hua..? Phone kyu kiya..." Someone spoke over a call using a voice changer.

" Boss!! Yaha do log aaye the...lagta hai police wale hi honge...wo uss ghatna par investigation shuru kar rahe hai..." The same man at Iqbal's shop spoke.

" Thik hai...koi plan sochna hoga...accha kaam kiya tumne...khabar dete rehna..." The boss spoke and ended the call.

Here the whole conversation was heard by Anubhav and Santosh as they had secretly planted a microphone at Iqbal's shop.

" Sir ye aadmi jise boss keh raha tha usne toh voice effect laga kar baat ki hai..." Santosh said.

" Koi baat nhi hum thoda toh kareeb jaa chuke hai...usse bhi jald pakad lenge..." Anubhav said in determined tone.

Anubhav and Santosh reached their hometown!!!

Iqbaal and Badnaam had still kept the respect of MPT placing the photo frame of its officers!!!

Who's the person behind the phone call and the suspicious person's boss?

To know keep reading" THE AFTERMATH "

Do vote & comment.

"Remember votes & comments, motivate me to write the next part early "

" Votes & Comments are key to early & interesting updates "

~ Kishaaa

Investigation

Author's POV

7 days more passed!!

The news of case reopening ran like the wind all over Lucknow.The mastermind behind the blast were to alerted.Anubhav was right they were still cautious at every step of them even though the incident had happened months back.To be safe Anubhav and Santosh had not contacted Chakorgao as they had no idea about the criminal's plan.

Anubhav & Santosh were at MPT investigating.The last 7 days they didn't do any movement in the case just to irritate the criminal.They were asking each & every shop if anybody knew anything.________________

" Yaha pein koi CCTV bhi nhi hai..." Santosh sadly said.

" Hota bhi toh...woh thodi usse rehna dete..." Anubhav said looking at the upward direction squinting his eyes due to the sun's heat.

" Chaliye thodi der visharam karte hai...dhup bohot hai...Kya pata aap kali pad gyi toh sab hume daatenge..." Anubhav said to Santosh and she giggled.

" Sir aap tension matt lijiye maine bhar bhar ke sunscreen lagaya hai...chahe toh kalse aapko bhi de dungi...nai toh madam sir hume daatengi ki humne unke Anu ko kal bana diya..." Santosh said.

" Kehne ke liye Haseenaji jeevit toh honi chahiye..." Anubhav turned the tables as he noticed someone's stare at him.

" I am sorry..." Santosh too acted.

Refreshing their mind with two cups of badnaam special the,the duo started their work again.

" Arre bhaisahab aap...!!" The same panipuri guy stopped Anubhav.

" Kya haal chaal ..." Anubhav approached towards him.

" Kya uss ek dinn hi aaye aap...phir ka nafrat hogayi chat se..." The man said.

" Nai nai...chat se kaun nafrat karega...wo bas kaam mein vyast hogaye..." Anubhav said.

" Waise...un madam ke thane ke saath bohot bura hua...bohot khyaal rakhti thi...hum thele walo ka..." The man sadly said.

" Ussi ki tehkikaat karne aaye hum...jald uss apradhi ko pakad lenge..." Anubhav said.

" Aap jante hai uss ghatna ke baare mein kuch bhi..." Anubhav questioned.

" Hum kya janenge...Bas akbaar se pata chala..." The man said.

" Koi nai...abhi khila dijiye do plate golgappe.." Anubhav said rubbing his hands in excitement.

" Khayengi na aap santosh..." Anubhav asked.

" Sir golgappe ko koi mana bhi kar sakta hai kya..." Santosh agreed.

" Sach kahe...aapki aur Haseena madam ki bohot acchi jodi lagti thi...tha kya kuch aap dono ke beech...?" The man asked boldly.

" Aisa hi kuch samaj lijiye " Anubhav said putting a golgappa in his mouth.

" Boss...ye aadmi toh golgappa khane lag gaya..." A man roaming on the street same as Anubhav and Santosh informed his boss.

" Aree wo pehle se golgappo ke liye pagal hai...piccha karte rehna...aur mujhe pal pal ki khabare chahiye..." The boss ordered.

" Ji boss..." The man replied.

" Chalte hai sahab..." Anubhav paid his fare and the duo left.

" Sir mujhe kuch yaad aaya..." Santosh happily said.

" Kya..." Anubhav confusedly asked.

" Sir jab madam sir urmila bani thi tab unhone ek case ke chalte ke light pole par camera lagaya tha...aur i am sure uss criminal ko kuch pata nhi hoga uss camera ke baare mein..." Santosh exclaimed.

" Dekha golgappe ka jaadu...chaliye jaldi..." Anubhav said and they rushed to the place.

(Assume the pole nearby MPT)

" Boss..inhe kisi cctv ke baare pata chala hai..." The man instanly alerted the boss.

" Piche piche jao...unke...I will see further " The boss ordered.

Anubhav and Santosh reached the spot and luckily they found the CCTV.

" Par iske liya aapko thane ka laptop chahiye hoga..." Anubhav said.

" Nhi sir isme ek memory card hai..bas wo nikalna hoga..." Santosh confidently said.

" Hum abhi laate hai..." Anubhav said and got ready to climb the pole.

" Sir risky hai...kisi electrician ko bula lete hai..." Santosh said.

" Utna wakt nhi hai humare paas...abhi tak uss apradhi tak ye baat pohoch bhi hyi hogi...wo isse yaha nhi rehne dega..." Anubhav said still looking up at the camera.

" Aap yhi rahiye hum aate hai..." Anubhav said calming Santosh.

Anubhav had just covered a distance less then half when bullet noise was heard.

The bullet directly hitted the camera destroying it.The next bullet slightly hitted on Anubhav's arm but luckily it just touched (chuu ke nikal gyi..)

" Sirrrr...." Santosh screamed.

" Hum thik hai..." Anubhav said jumping of the pole swiftly, covering the wound.

" Aap jaiye usse pakadiye..." Anubhav said in pain and Santosh ran after the person.

The person had covered face with black mask leaving no gap to recognize. And body covered in Black jumpsuit.

" Rukko..." Santosh said throwing 5 stones back to back in the culprit's way.

The culprit got stumbled while missing the stones to run and falled off on the ground.

Santosh quickly approached the culprit and grabbed hands.The culprit seeing chance pushed Santosh to ground and ran.

" Nhi rok paayi usse..." Santosh came huffing towards Anubhav.

" Bass ye bangle mila hai..." Santosh said giving a silver bangle to Anubhav.

" Ye toh qayamat ka hai...!" Both said examining the bangle.

" Matlab Haseena ji sahi iske picche qayamat hai..." Anubhav said remembering Haseena's words.

" Ha..." Santosh agreed.

" Sir khoon beh raha hai aapke haato se...chaliye pehle ghar..." Santosh immediately took him home Anubhav had to listen else she would directly complain Haseena.___________

" Bohot chot lagi hai aapko sir...agar madam sir ne dekhliya toh gadbad hojayegi.." Santosh said cleaning the wound.

" Hume aadat hai inn sabki...aap chinta mat kijiye...Joh hota hai acche ke liye hota hai...ye chot jarur mili par hume uss apraadhi ka naam bhi toh pata chala.." Anubhav said to his worried sister while Santosh gave an angry look.

" Hogaya..." Santosh said.

" Laiyye...hum aapko laga dete hai..." Anubhav said seeing a wound on Santosh's hand.

" Nai..mai laga lungi..." Santosh denied.

" hume gyaat hai...aap nhj lagayengi...dijiye.." Anubhav took the first aid kit from her.

" Aa...aah...dhire kariye na..." Santosh winced.

" Ha...maaf kijiye..." Anubhav slowly covered her hand with a bandage.

Santosh hugged Anubhav.

" Accha hua aapko goli jor se nhi lagi..." Santosh said with tears in her eyes.

" Shaant hojaiye...hum thik hai..." Anubhav said tapping her forehead.

The duo finally came across the culprit!!

Haseena's guess was right it was Rani the fake qayamat!!

How will the duo find Rani?

How will Haseena react on seeing Anubhav and Santosh's wounds?

To know keep reading" THE AFTERMATH "

Do vote & comment.

"Remember votes & comments, motivate me to write the next part early "

" Votes & Comments are key to early & interesting updates "

~ Kishaaa

Mithïi

<hr>

A uthor's POV

Anubhav & Santosh were still in Lucknow planning to arrest Rani asap.On the side of Chakorgao Nobody had clue about what was happening in Lucknow!A few days before Anubhav had messaged Mihir about the duo being okay but not about the case's progress.

Here Karishma developed a great bond with the little girl on her window .The girl visited her early in morning giving her the bappa's prasaad.___
___

" Ye chutki abhi tak kahe nhi aayi..." Karishma thought as the time had passed when the girl arrived daily.

" Thik toh hogi na wo..." Karishma's concern rose.

" Chalo karu...nashta taiyaar hai..." Mihir called Karishma.

" Ji patidev..." Karishma said closing the window and went out.

All were chit-chatting randomly when the door be rang.

" Dhyaan se kholna..." Haseena advised.

Shivani opened the door a little and peeped out finding no one.Her eyes travelled down to see the same little girl standing there.

" Tum yaha kya kar rhi ho..." Shivani asked but the girl looked down.

" Bolegi bhi ya nhi..." Shivani again asked.

" Aandar aa tu pehle..." Shivani said holding her hand and got her in and closed the door.

" Ab bol ye muh kyu latka rakha hai..." Shivani asked while others looked at her confused.

" Ye yaha kya kar rhi hai...ye toh shivani je saamne aane se darti hai...phir aaj ghar tak kaise pohoch gyii..." Karishma thought.

" Unhone mujhe dikaal diya aasharam se..." The girl said.

" Matlab...wo aisa kyu karenge..." Shivani questioned.

" Pata nhi...lagta hai uss pintya ne kuch bol diya hoga unn ko..." The girl said.

" Tu ye tera saaman lekar kyu ghum rhi hai..." Shivani said as she had a bedsheet with clothes in it.

" Toh kya karu...mere paas rehne ke liye kaha jagah hai...raat toh maine asharam ke bahar kat di...par unhone subah mujhe phir hakaal diya..." The girl explains.

" Thik hai tu ye rakh yaha...yaha reh le...mai baat karti hu unse..." Shivani said.

" Mat lag unke muh abhi...mujhe nhi rehna waha...unlogo ko meri izzat hi nhi hai...isiliye mai nhi ja ungi waha..." The girl announced making everyone gasp at her talks.

" Meri vajah se unhe aachar milta tha...ab unhe wo bina namak wala khana khana padega..." The girl said with attitude.

" Tu mere liye koi accha dusra asharam dhund de...mai waha chali jaungi..." The girl said.

" Kaun hai ye Shivani..." Pushpaji asked.

" Ye hai Mithi yhi chakorgao ke aashram mein rehti hai...acchi dosti hai humari..." Shivani said holding Mithi's chin and shaking her face with fun.

" Lekin iske naam pein mat jaana...naam iska mithi hai patmr bohot tikhi hai ye...agar koi isse ek bolega toh ye usse char suna kar aajayegi..." Shivani introduced Mithi.

" Woh toh dikha hi...inhe izzat shabd ka meaning kitni acchi tareke se pata hai..." Haseena said smiling and looking at Mithi.

" Jaa tu mere kamre mein.. muh dhole..." Shivani said and Mithi ran towards her room and secretly blinked at Karishma.

" Tu kaise jaanti hai isse jiji.." Binni asked.

" 2 saal ki thi jab iski maa ne isse mujhe saupa tha...cancer se lad rhi thi iski maa aur iska baba toh iske janam hote hi kuch mahino mein ek accident mein mare gye... Phir maine isse yaha aasharam mein chod diya...Tab toh iski shakal dekh ke iska naam Mithi rakha maine par ye toh teekhi mirchi nikli..." Shivani chuckled at last.

" Par ab kya...usse toh nikal diya asharam se..." Karishma asked.

" Ab woh toh yaha nhi rehna chahti isiliye dusra dhund na hoga...tab tak yhi rahegi..." Shivani sadly said.

" Matlab do do teekhi mirchiyon ko sambhalna padega..." Billu secretly whispered to Cheetah.

" Abe ka maja aata hai...karishma madam suni na toh ek thapad laga den gi.." Cheetah whispered back.

" Wahi toh maara hi nhi hai unhone mujhe jabse yaha hai hum..." Billu sadly said

Mihir's phone rang.

" Anubhav ka call hai..." Mihir said.

" Baat kar sakte hai..? safe haina..." Anubhav asked

" Ji..." Mihir answered back.

" Toh hume uss shaks ka pata chal gaya hai...Rani hi hai wo...ab bas usstak jald se jald pohochna hai..." Anubhav said making everyone shock.

" Aap dono thik hai na..." Cheetah asked.

" Ha hum dono thik hai...santosh aaram kar rhi hai..." Anubhav said.

" Rakhte hai...nai toh kisi ko shak hojayega..." Anubhav ended the call.

" waise ye rani hai kaun...? " Amar asked.

" Pucchiye mat tin baar saza kat kar aayi hai..mye chouthi baar hai...joh hume pareshaan kar rhi hai..." Pushpaji said.

" Matlab hum sahi the...par ye intna bada crime kyu karegi...kuch toh vajah hogi..." Haseena thoughtfully said.

" Vajah kuch bhi ho...iss baar faasi karwa kar rahenge hum..." A angry Karishma said______________

Author's POV

The day soon ended!Everyone was now at relief knowing about the person who destroyed their lives.They were now determined to punish Rani badly.

Here,Mithi spoke to no one but spent her whole day complaning about the asharam.She wished to speak to Karishma but didn't as she got no chance.

It was night time and everyone had just finished their dinner and sitting together.____________

" Shivani mai so ungi kaha..." Mithi asked.

" Kaha matlab...itna bada vada hai...koi bhi kamre mein soja..." Shivani said.

" Par mujhe akele darr lagta hai....Ashram mein kittu didi le saath soti thi..." Mithi said.

" Toh...? " Shivani asked.

" Mai inke saath so jau...? " Mithi asked pointing towards Karishma.

" Par.. inke saath ye inkrme husband bhi hai..." Shivani said referring Mihir.

" Aree aap toh wahi haina...uss din aapne mujhe chocolate do thi....station par..." Mithi said looking at Mihir.

" Ohh...toh wo tum thi...mera dhyaan hi nhi gaya..." Mihir said.

" Toh mai kya aap dono ke saath so sakti hu...?" Mithi asked.

" Ha bilkul kyu nhi...." Mihir said pulling her cheek.

" Dekha inhe koi poblem nhi hai..." Mithi said to Shivani.

" Toh thik hai..." Shivani agreed.

" Tum inke sath jao...mai aata hu..." Mihir asked Mithi to go with Karish ma.____________

" Jhoot bolke ruki ho yaha...? " Karishma questioned Mithi as they entered in the room.

" Nai..sachmein uss pintya ne meri shikayat kar di aashram ki madam se...ki mai roz subah yaha teri khidki mai aake timepass karti hu...." Mithi explained.

" Par isme galat kya hai..." Karishma asked.

" Mai nashte ke liye der se pohochti hu na...isiliye chupke andar ghusna padta hai...aur wo pintya ne dekh liya tha...isiliye mujhe nikal diya..." Mithi said.

" Accha meri wajah se tumhe asharam se nikal diya...maaf kardo mujhe.." Karishma apologized.

" Aap load mat lo...shivani hai na wo mere liye dusra aasharam dhund degi...phir mein waha reh lungi...Shivani bohot acchi hai.." Mithi said.

" Accha thik hai...ye tumhare haatho ko kya hua hai..." Karishma said looking at her arms.

" Kuch nhi kal asharam ke bag (बाग) mein soyi thi...toh macharo ne kaat liya..." Mithi said looking at her rashes.

" Ruko...hum dawai laate hai..." Karishma said getting up and grabbed a ointment from the table.

Karishma applied the ointment all over Mithi's arms.

" Thank you..." Mithi thanked.

" Ab chalo sojao..." Karishma said.

" Hmm.." Mithi said taking a bedsheet and started making her bed on floor.

" Ye kya kar rhi ho..." Karishma asked confused.

" Sone ki taiyaari..." Mithi casually said.

" Waha kyu yaha upar aao..." Karishma said

" Par upar aap dono soyenge..." Mithi said

" Par tum thodi itni badi jagah logi..hum tino aaram se sojayenge..." Karishma said and Mithi climbed the bed.

" Aap bohot acchi ho..." Mithi said hugging Karishma leaving her shocked.

" Ab sojaye...?" Karishma asked.

" Hmm..." Mithi said and slept beside Karishma.

As a tired Mithi layed down sleep took over her.Karishma was still awake waiting for Mihir as he was busy checking everyone's vitals.

" Tum abhi tak jaag rhi ho..." Mihir asked entering the room.

" Ha..." Karishma said.

" Kya hua...kuch soch rhi ho..." Mihir asked.

" Hmmm..." Karishma asked.

" Kya hua..." Mihir asked keeping his hand on her hairs caressing her.

" Bhagwaan baccho ki bhi kitni buri pariksha lete hai na...Iss bacchi ko hi dekh lijiye...kitni choti hai...pehle maa baap ka saaya uth gaya aur ab usse uske aasharam se bhi nikaal diya..." Karishma said adoring a sleeping Mithi.

" Woh toh hai...Phir bhi dekho kitni bahadur hai..." Mihir said seeing Mithi.

" Ab sojao...der tak jagna thik nhi hai..." Mihir said.

" Hmm..." Karishma said and closed her eyes.____________

" Hume yaad kyu nhi aaraha wo locket....humne wo rani ke paas toh nhi dekha...par phir wo waha pohocha kaise...koi aur shaamil toh nhi iss mein...." Haseena tried to remember the Samosa locket's owner .

" Inhe hum kaise bhul gaye...ye shaks bhi toh uss sab mein shaamil ho sakta hai...hume 100% yakeen ye locket unhi ka hai..." Haseena finally remembered.

Here was Mithi's story!!

Haseena finally remembered the locket's owner!!

What do you think who is the owner?

To know keep reading" THE AFTERMATH "

Do vote & comment.

"Remember votes & comments, motivate me to write the next part early "

" Votes & Comments are key to early & interesting updates "

~ Kishaaa

Evil Returns

A bonus update because I am Happyyyy

Wo kyu last mein dekh lena.

" Ye pendant Genda ka hai...humse wo kaise chut gyi...par Anubhav ka kehna hai ki wo sab Rani ka kiya dhara hai...phir Genda ka ye pendant waha kaise pohocha...kahi ye doni ki mili milaayi saazish nhi..." Haseena jumped out of bed sensing her thoughts.

" Aur der nhi karni chahiye hume jaldi se Anubhav se contact karna hoga..." Haseena said and to Mihishma room.

" Patidev darwaaza kholiye na..." Karishma said as she heard a knock.

" Raat ko kaun aayega..." Mihir questioned.

" Bhoot aaya bhoot aaya..." Mithi murmured and snuggled into Karishma.

" Bhoot....? " Karishma opened her eyes and saw Mithi snuggled into her.

" Accha ye bad badayi..." Karishma smiled.

" Darwaaza kholiye na Mihir...." Karishma said shaking Mihir.

" Raat ko bhi sone nhi dete..." Mihir complained getting up.

" Haseena tum yaha iss wakt..." Mihir asked.

" Ha wo hume Anubhav se baat karni hai jaldi..." Haseena said.

" Hum laga denge phone par itni raat ko... kuch pareshaani hai kya..." Mihir asked.

" Wo bas hume uss locket ke baare mein kuch pata chala hai...hume woh unhe jaldi batana hai..." Haseena hurriedly said.

" Aao andar...lagate hai hum phone..." Mihir said and Haseena followed him in.

" Madam sir aap yaha...itni raat ko..." Karishma got up seeing her.

" Ha wo Hume wo locket kiska hai pata chal gaya hai..Aur isiliye Anubhav se contact karna hai..." Haseena said to Karishma.

" Kaun hai..." Karishma asked.

" Genda..." Haseena answered in despair.

" Matlab wo...dono ka kaam hai.." Karishma concluded.

" Ha...rani akele ye nhi kar sakti na toh uske paas power hai na paisa...genda ko shaamil karliya..." Haseena said.

" Hello Anubhav..hume bohot jaruri baat karni hai aapse..." Haseena said.

" Ha...parantu...aap bohot pareshaan lag rhi hai aap thik hai...?" Anubhav said sensing her voice.

" Anubhav wo locket kisi aur ka nhi genda ka hai...inn sab mein genda bhi shaamil hai..." Haseena said making Anubhav shocked.

" Ha Anubhav hume pura yakeen hai ki wo locket genda ka hai..." Haseena confidently said.

" Accha kiya aapne abhi bata diya...hum kuch karte jaldi unn tak pohoch ne ke liye..." Anubhav said in a serious tone.

" Dhyaan se Anubhav wo dono bohot khatarnaak hai...kuch bhi kar sakti hai..." Haseena alerted him.

" Ji..shubh ratri..." Anubhav wished.

" Good night " Haseena wished back and disconnected the phone.

" Par hum uss genda tak kaise pohochenge..." Karishma asked.

" Kuch bhi karke hume uss tak pohochna hoga...Aur hum iss baar unhe faansi chadhakar hi manenge..." Haseena said in a determined tone.

Rani with Genda is involved in the crime!!

How will they reach till the Evil duo?

To know keep reading" THE AFTERMATH "

Do vote & comment.

"Remember votes & comments, motivate me to write the next part early "

" Votes & Comments are key to early & interesting updates "

~ Kishaaa

A happy news i want to share is our story THE AFTERMATH had ranked #1 in Anuseena and many more other ranks.This is what i wanted to achieve.

Thank you to all my readers!!The ones who commented sweet reviews about the parts and also to the ones who voted.I also thank my silent readers as they to contribute in this achievement.

Grateful!!!

Critical

A uthor's POV

Today was happy sunday morning.In Lucknow,Anubhav and Santosh had decided to spend their Sunday with kids on the playground.Of course! They had a mission motive.A clue from Anubhav's detective was to be received today.

Santosh and Anubhav reached the ground at sharp 7 in the morning.The energy of the kids motivated them to another level of extent.Soon they took their positions and the game began.___________

" Jivan kuch din baccho ke saath bhi guzarlene chahiye bohot anand aata hai..." Anubhav said enjoying the game.

" Sir...toh phir jab aapki aur madam sir ki shaadi hojayegi aur aapke babies aajayenge toh...thode kya aapka pura jivan ussi mein jayega..." Santosh's innocence was at peak.

" Aapko subah subah hi humne singhade ka halwa diya tha...khaya nhi aapne.." Anubhav sarcastically spoke.

" Khaya na bohot accha bana tha...aur ye joh bola na maine wo maasumiyat nhi tha....Pure hosh mein bola hai maine...." Santosh said with an extra sweet smile and continued playing.

" Kaha phas gaye hum...!!" Anubhav facepalmed himself.

" Anubhav sir...niche jhukiye...ball lag jayegi..." Santosh yelled at Anubhav who was resting as not to hurt his wound again.

Anubhav catched the ball easily saving himself from it.

" Baccho ye ball kharab hogayii hai...dusri ball se khelna..." Anubhav said.

Anubhav unwrapped the upper layer of plastic from the ball and found a chit stuck with a note written.

" Ghode godown ke picchu...Chikku ke ped ke nicchu..." He read the note.

" Ye paheli de diye tum titu..." Anubhav said thinking about the riddle.

" Santosh Sharma..." Anubhav called her.

" Kya sir abhi mai out karne hi wali thi usse..." Santosh unwillingly came to him.

"Ye padhiye...isme se kuch pata chalta hai kya dekhiye..." Anubhav said handing over the cheat to Santosh.

" Ye kaisi bhasha hai..." Santosh said in confusion.

" Hindi hi hai..." Anubhav said.

" Ha aapki wali nhi hai...isiliye laga nhi hindi hai..." Santosh sarcastically said.

" Pata hai aapko ghode bazaar kaha hai..." Anubhav asked.

" Ha..." Santosh said.

" Chaliye phir..." Anubhav said and they got into the car and left.________

______

" Ye gaadi kyu ruk gyi..." Santosh said as the car stopped urgently.

" Lagta hai chedchani ki hai kisi ne...Gaadi se bahar nhi nikalna..." Anubhav instructed.

Anubhav messaged his detective about the change of plan and shared his live location asking to send police force when given a signal.

" Ye unn logo ki saazish hai...hum car se utrenge aur ye log hume le jayen ge..." Anubhav whispered.

" Abhi...abhi kya karenge hum..." Santosh asked

" Niche utrenge...aur phir jo hoga dekha jayega...inse unn tak pohoch toh payenge..." Anubhav said.

" Chaliye...par aise bilkul nhi lagna chahiye ki hume ye sab gyat hai...gaadi check karne ke bahane se utriye..." Anubhav said and both got down.

Getting down Anubhav opened the car's docket and Santosh acted to check it.When suddenly they were hitted by iron rods on their head instantly making them unconsious.

The two goons made them smell high power chloroform.Destroying there phone's and throwing it there they carried unconsious Anubhav and Santosh in a car and further to their secret place.____________

" Bade aaye dono...hum tak pohochne ka plan banaye the....ab khud upar wale tak pohochenge..." Genda laughed in evil tone looking towards Anubhav and Santosh who were unconsciously tied on the chairs.

" Madam chloroform bohot high dose mein gaya hai...4-5 din tak hosh toh aayega hi nhi..." One the man said.

" Accha hai...waise bhi tadapa tadapa ke maarna dono ko..." Rani smirked.

———————

Author's POV

Here at Chakorgao nobody had idea about what was happening in Luckn ow.The last contact with them was when Haseena told them about Genda which happened a before.Everyone were tensed but decided to be positive and wish better.

Here, Mithii was fully attached to everyone.Mihishma had developed a parent like bond with Mithii.But whenever they decided to talk about Mithii's adoption to Shivani,Mithii would get excited about her new o rphanage.Hence they felt Mithii would except them.___________

" Yaha humse itne bade hai....phir bhi humse subah utha nhi jaata...Aur ye teekhi mirchi subah mandir hoke bhi aagayii..." Billu said still in sleepy tone.

" Aree narbakshi vanar kuch toh seekh bacchi se..." Cheetah teased Billu.

" Uski bachpan se aadat hai...pehle jab choti thi toh ek uske aasharam ki Aaji thi woh lejaya karti thi usse mandir...phir wo guzar gyi...par Mithii ne wo aadat chodi nhi roz mandir jaati hai..." Shivani praised Mithi.

" Ha...uss din humare liye line mein khade hokar prasaad layi thi...taaki hum jaldi thik hojaye..." Karishma said with a smile.

" Aap jiske baare mein baat kar rahe hai kaha hai wo...kaha hai Mithii..." Haseena asked as Mithii wasn't with them.

" Aaa..." A voice was heard from the kitchen making everybody rush towards kitchen.

As they rushed to the kitchen they found Mithi standing on the kitchen worktop with a bleeding finger.Haseena quickly picked her and made her sit on a chair.

" Mithii...dard horaha hai..." Karishma said cupping her face.

" N..nai..." Mithii lied.

" Mai first aid leke aati hu..." Shivani said and was about to go but Mihir stopped.

" Nai..ruko hum hi Mithii ko le chalte hai room mein...chaku laga hai isse infection na phaila ho..." Mihir wished.

Everyone were tensed for Mithii but Mithii showed no sign of pain over her face.

Taking Mithii to the room..Mihir made her sit on the bed.Only Haseena,Karishma with Mithii and Mihir were present.

" Mai thik hu...bass ye khoon poch do..." Mithi said in a shivering voice.

" Chup raho...dikha raha kitna thik ho...kitna khoon beh raha hai..." Karishma scolded scaring Mithii as it was the first time she heard high tone.

" Karishma singh shaant bacchi hai wo...darr rhi hai..." Haseena calmed her.

Mihir took Mithii's hand and washed the blood out of her finger but the blood was still oozing out.With a great effort Mihir wiped all the blood and stopped its flow.As the wound was clean Mihir saw a big cut on her finger.

Mihir applied a antiseptic gel over it at which Mithii hissed in pain.Karishma quickly embraced Mithii in a loving hug and held her near her chest which made Mithii teary for the first time.But Mithii didn't let her tears flow out.

Mihir covered her finger with a cotton and wrapped a bandage around it.He signalled Haseena to bring his another bag as it was needed.Taking out a syringe and filling it up with medicine.Mihir looked towards Mithii who had hid her face in Karishma's chest closing her eyes.While seeing the syringe Karishma closed her eyes holding Mithii tightly.

As Mihir injected,Mithi hissed in pain bitting her lower lips and controlling her tears.

Mihir applied some gel over it and pressed it with a cotton.

Haseena,Mihir and Karishma were tensed seeing no emotion of pain.Was she holding her tears!!But why?? was the only thing they thought.

As the medication was done Karishma made Mithii lay down on the bed covering her with a comforter.

" Karu tum yhi raho..." Saying so Mihir left and Haseena followed him giving assuring look to Karishma.___

" Shivani Mithii kitne saal ki hai..." Mihir asked Shivani in a worried tone.

" 8 saal ki...par kyu kuch hua hai kya..." Shivani asked tensed.

" Haa..." Mihir said in tensed tone.

" Shivani abhi usse itni chot lagi thi par usse dard nhi hua...andar Mihir ne usse injection lagaya par usne kuch react nhi kiya...Aisa kaise kaise ho sakta hai...usse kuch toh hua hoga...Aur wo chot choti nhi thi bohot bada cut laga hai usse...dard hua hoga na..." Haseena said in a confused tone.

" Nai...usse dard hua hai...bas wo apna dard chupa rhi hai..." Mihir said.

" Wo jab koi aansu pochne wala na hona...toh insaan rona bhul jaata hai...wahi hua hain Mithii ke saath...yaha ke aashram wale usse pasand nhi karte hai...bas isliye kyunki woh shaitaan hai...isiliye uspar koi dhyaan nhi deta...mujhe ye baat pata nhi thi...nhi toh mai usse kab ka Mumbai le jaati..." Shivani emotionally explained.

" Bacchi hai wo...abhi apna dard nhi dikhayegi toh kaise chalega..." Pushpaji said in a worried tone.

" Par hum ye ignore nhi kar sakte...Aage chalke usse in sabse mental health problems ho sakti hai...hume samjhana hoga usse..." Mihir said.

" Nai samjhegi wo...Bohot baar bola hai maine usse ki chot lage toh batati ja...par wo bas ye keh ke taal deti hai ki ' Mithii bohot takadwaan hai usse dard nhi hota '...isiliye toh mai usse har wakt ped par chadne se rokti hu...taaki aur chot na aaye..." Shivani said almost in tears.

" Mai aati hu...uske orphanage walo ka phone aaya tha wo aarahe the kal lene...thode din baad bula lenge..." Shivani said getting up.

" Nai Shivani ruko..." Cheetah stopped her.

" Humare khyaal se unko aane do.." Cheetah said.

" Par wo bimar hai...usse bukhaar bhi aasakta hai...wo travel nhi karsakti..." Mihir said the fact but Mihir too didn't wanted to let Mithii go.

" Nhi Mihir bhaiya...agar Mithii ke emoson bahar lane hai na toh aane dijiye unhe...hum sab jante hai wo yaha kitni ghulmil gyi hai...aur hum bhi...khaas karke aap aur Karishma madam..." The psychologist Cheetah said.

" Ha...karishma toh aise uska khyaal rakhti hai jaise usse apna...khoya hua baccha wapas mil gaya ho..." Pushpaji said emotionally.

" Dekhiye...hum bol rahe unhe aane dijiye...hum batate hai...hum psychology pade hai...Mithii nhi jaana chahtii sabko chodke...agar kal hum usse bhejenge na toh pakka wo apne emoson bahar layegii...vishwas kijiye hum par..." Cheetah confidently said.

"Good Cheetah.... Thik toh keh rahe ho tum..aane unn logo ko..." Mihir said to Shivani and praised Cheetah.

The same plan was conveyed to Karishma.___________

The evening passed but a silent one as Mithii distanced herself from everyone on knowing that she will be now moving to a new orphanage.

" Ye dekh...kal aarahe hai tere naye ashaaram wale tujhe lene...jaldi uth ja na..." Shivani said entering the room with a packed bag of Mithii's clothes.

" Kaha pein hai naya aashram...?" Mithii asked in a not so happy mood.

" Mumbai...." Shivani answered.

" Chalo Mithii hum tumhara khana laaye hai..." Karishma said bringing her dinner.

" Aap yaha rakh do mai kha lungi khud se...kalse aap nhi honge mujhe khilane.." Mithii hurtfully said.

Karishma looked at Shivani to which Shivani gave assuring look.

Karishma placed the plate infront of Mithii and then the medicine packet.

" Ye dawaiyya bhi le lena hum nhi honge kalse " Karishma said and left the room.________

At night,Mithii had already slept on the floor before Mihishma entered the room.

Mihishma's heart pained but they had to let it be for betterment of Mithii.

At middle of night..Mihishma's unstable sleep broke as they heard Mithi murmuring in sleep.What she was murmuring was not heard but she was scared.Mihir picked her and placed her in between them and checked her temperature which was obviously high.

As Karishma carressed Mithii's hairs this helped calming down Mithii and her murmuring stopped.While Mihir wiped of the sweat over her face.

Mithii slept peacefully in the comfort of her to be parents.

No one has a clue of what's happening in Lucknow!!

Anubhav and Santosh are kidnapped!!

How will they come out of the evil's trap!!!

Will Mithii go to her new orphanage or will Cheetah's plan be successful?

To know keep reading" THE AFTERMATH "

Do vote & comment.

"Remember votes & comments, motivate me to write the next part early "

" Votes & Comments are key to early & interesting updates "

~ Kishaaa

Angel

- -

I had a doubt!!Are you all loving the Mithii track??Kyonki i know agar pura focus case pein dalte toh bohot boring hojata isiliye maine Mithii ko add kiya!!Hoping that you are not finding it off track!!Let me know in the comments.

Happy Reading_____________

Author's POV

The next day began with a uncanny silence.The whole Pawar Vada was silent and sad.Mithii who always used to wake up early in the morning was still sleeping tensing the atmosphere in Pawar Vada.________

" Mithii....uth..subah hogayi hai..." Shivani tried to wake her up.

Mithi rubbing her eyes woke up and looked around her surroundings.

" Main...itni der tak soyi...aur yaha upar kaise phonchi..." Mithii said confused.

" Wo sab chod...jaldi taiyaar hoja..pata hai na aaj tujhe mumbai jaana hai. ..ek ghante mein nikalna hai..hume wo log intezaar karenge station par..." Shivani said examining Mithii's change of expression.

" Thik hai...mein abhi taiyaar hoke aati hu..." Mithii said and folding her blanket.

Author's POV

As Mithii got ready she came to the hall where all were having there breakfast.Her eyes searched for Mihishma but they were nowhere to be seen.

Mithii silently sat down and had her breakfast.All were really sad seeing Mithii silent.From the last one week the Pawar was lit up with laughter due to Mithii naughtiness.______________

" Mai mandir hoke aati hu..." Mithii informed Shivani and departed.

" Mujhe bilkul accha nhi lag raha...kaisi shaant hogai hai teekhi mirchi.." Billu said missing her naughtiness.

" Thodi der aur ruko bille...kahi nhi jaegi ye " Cheetah said.

Author's POV

Mithii returned from the temple with something in her hand.She entered the house but with a smile.________

" Apna haath aage karo..." Mithii instructed Pushpaji.

Pushpaji did as instructed and forwarded her hand.Mithii tied a red thread around her wrist and touched her feet.Pushpaji was touched by her action but controlled her emotions.

" Aap apna haath aage karo..." Mithii said to Haseena and Haseena did.

" Aapki hasi bohot acchi hai..." Mithi said tieing the thread while Haseena hugged her.

Mithii tied the thread to everyone Amar,Cheetah,Billu,Binni and Shivani.

Mithii glanced at the two threads remaining for Mihishma and fisted it in her hands and walked to the room.

Mithii returned with her bag and kept it at the door.

" Hume nhi bandhogi dhaaga..." Mihishma asked.

Mithi turned around hearing the voices she wished and approached them.

" Laayi toh thi mai...par aap dono dikhe hi nhi..." Mithi said.

" Ab toh haina ab bandho..." Mihir said forwarding his hand.

Mithii tied the thread on his wrist and smiled looking at him.

Mithii just looked at Karishma and Karishma forwarded her hand.

No one from the trio spoke a word.

" Chale Mithii..." Shivani asked.

" Hmmm..." Mithii said.

Shivani opened the door and lifted Mithi's another bag in her hand kept it outside.

" Mai gaadi ki chabi leke aati hu..." Shivani said and got in while Mithii stood their.

" Kuch hua...?" Karishma asked with a hope.

" Nai...." Shivani disappointedly said.

Shivani grabbed the keys and went out while everyone watched them secretly.

" Kya hua tu shaant kyu hai subah se..." Shivani asked Mithii.

" Kuch nhi..." Mithii said and walked towards the car.

" Tu jaana chahti haina...mumbai..." Shivani asked.

" Ha...tu aisa kyu puch rhi hai...chal jaldi wo log ruke hue hai.." Mithii said and holded her hand.

" Ha..." Shivani said and turned back and nodded negatively looking at everyone.

" Shayad wo nhi rukna chahti yaha..." Mihir sadly said.

" Toh woh itni...shaant kyu hogai hai kalse..." Haseena added.

" Shayad...uski chot ki wajah se kamzori hogi..." Mihir said.

Karishma not able to control her tears ran to her room and Mihir followed her.

Here,Shivani and Mithii went off to the railway station.

" Tu utar niche mein...laati hu saamaan..." Shivani said, while thinking something Mithii got down.

" Chal wo rahe wo samane...tere aasharam ke naye log..." Shivani pointed at two women.

" Chalo..." Mithii said.

Shivani and Mithii walked towards the women.

" Thik se...rehna.." Shivani said bending at Mithii's height.

" Aur...call karti rehna..inke paas hai mera number..." Shivani said carressing her cheek.

" Hmmm....toh rona mat..." Mithii wiped her tears and hugged her.

" Nai roungi...tu khyaal rakhna khud ka...Mai aajaungi Mumbai thode dino mein..." Shivani smiled.

" hmm..." Mithii said and one of the women holded her hand and they departed to their train.

Shivani was helpless she wanted to stop Mithii but something became a barrier in stopping her.

Author's POV

As Mithii settled herself on her seat her eyes travelled towards her neighbouring row.A mother feeding her child with all love and care.While the child's father talking to him.Seeing them all Mithii could remember was Karishma and Mihir.She smiled seeing them and a tear escaped her eyes. The mother made her child sleep on his chest and patted his forehead.This remembered Mithii of how comfortable she felt in Karishma's arms.It looked like Cheetah's plan was succeeding.Mithii suddenly feeling scared got up from her seat.___________

"

Kya hua beta..thik ho tum..." One of the orphanage lady asked.

Mithii once glanced at the sweet family.

" Nai...mujhe..jana..hai.." Mithii said in a shivering voice.

" Kaha jaana hai..." The lady said in a tensed voice.

" G..ghar...shivani...shivani kaha hai..." Mithii said peeping out of the window.

" Achanak kya hua tumhe...thik ho na..." The lady's concern rose.

" Shivani...Shivani..." Mithii ran towards the train door while the two ladies followed her.

Shivani who had a idea as given by Cheetah had waited till the train's departure.

" Shivani...shivani " Mithii searched for her while the ladies running behind her with her bags.

" Mithii...tu bahar kyu aayi..." Shivani said as she saw Mithii running.

" Shivani nai jaana mujhe Mumbai...mujhe nhi jaana...mujhe unn dono ke saath rehna hai..." Mithii hugged Shivani but still not crying but shivering.

" Accha nhi jana...koi baat nhi...pehle tu shaant hoja..." Shivani said taking her into her arms and calming her down.

" I am sorry...par ye nhi jana chahti..." Shivani apologized the ladies.

" Koi baat nhi...waise bhi iske marzi ke khilaaf nhi leja sakte hum ise...." The lady understandingly said.

" Ye saman....Hum chalte hai..." Another lady said and they both departed.

" Maine pucha tha tujhse...nai jana tha toh bata deti..." Shivani said taking Mithii back to car.

Shivani drew towards Pawar Vada. Mithii didn't speak a single word in the car.

As they reached,Shivani rang the bell and Haseena opened it.

Haseena smiled tearfully.

" Cheetah...tumhara plan kaam kar gaya...." Haseena said looking at the door.

" Aayein...? sachmein...?" Cheetah said coming to the door.

Everyone were delighted to see Mithii back with Shivani.

Author's POV

Mithii glanced at everyone's face but her eyes searched for some other face.Leaving her chappals Mithii ran inside looking for Karishma and Mihir.She rushed to their room and pushed it open.__________

" Amma...." Mithii shouted in tears.

Mihishma who were sitting their blankly got shocked seeing Mithii there.

The more shocked was Karishma on hearing Amma from her mouth.

" Mithii...." Mihishma came to Mithii.

" Mujhe nhi jaana tum dono ko chodke..." Mithii hugged both of them brusting into tears finally.

" Toh kyu gyi...pata hai kitna bura laga hume..." Karishma said tightening her hug.

" Bohot bura haal hua tha Mithii humara..." Mihir said breaking the hug and caressing Mithii.

" Sorry..." Mithii said still sobbing.

" Ab khi nhi jaane denge tumhe...humare saath rahogi tum..." Mihir said.

" Ha hum...tumhare hai...hum bohot pyaar karenge tumse..." Karishma said.

" Mere A...Amma P..papa...??" Mithii asked with in between her hiccups.

" Ha...aapke Amma-Papa..." Mihishma happily answered.

Karishma planted numerous kisses on Mithii's face.

While others tearfully adoring the newly formed family clapped on their reunion

----

Indeed Mithii is an angel sent by universe for Mihishma.

And a healer for Karishma due to loss of her baby.

Keep reading" THE AFTERMATH "

Do vote & comment.

"Remember votes & comments, motivate me to write the next part early "

" Votes & Comments are key to early & interesting updates "

~ Kishaaa

Closer

A uthor's POV

Yesterday was a the best day for Mihishma and family as Mithii finally concerned them as their parents.While the question non-contact with Anubhav and Santosh was yet to be solved!!___________

" Kitne dinn hogaya hai...kuch contact nhi ho pa raha hai...hume bohot darr lag raha hai..." Cheetah stated her fear.

" Ha...hume bhi bohot chinta horhi hai...na toh phone track ho paraha hai ya unka call lag raha hai..." Karishma said.

" Anubhav bhai na ek msg ya missed call dete...ki hum dono thik hai...ch inta mat kijiye " Haseena irritatedly said.

" Santuji bhi boli thi pal pal ki update dengi...kuch bhi nhi update de ri..." Cheetah sadly said.___________

Author's POV

The old godown was lightly dimmed.Anubhav and Santosh were still unconsciously tied on the chair.Anubhav's hand moved and adjusting to the surroundings he opened his eyes.Recalling the past events he finally remembered where he was and how close he was to the criminals.Anubhav looked beside Santosh who was still unconscious.The two men didn't get an idea of him being fine.Anubhav taking it as an advantage with a great difficulty stamped his feet for 3 times signalling his detective to be ready with a team as his shoes had micro device in it.___________

" Santosh sharma...uthiye..." Anubhav tried to wake Santosh up.

" Ohoo...jaag gye Anubhav babu..." Rani said walked towards him.

" Badi jaldi jaag gye...mujhe laga direct upar ki ticket katlii..." Genda said coming.

" Itni jaldi nhi...tum dono papo ki saza dekar hi hum upar ka ticket kaate nge..." Anubhav said in anger.

" Gussa na karo Anubhav babu..." Rani said leaning closer to him.

" Woh kya hai na...aapki premika ne humare premi ko maar dala...isiliye ye sab karna pada...Ab aapko kaise jinda chod sakte hai..." Rani said evily.

" Waise ek deal hai..." Rani said with smirk.

" Aapke paas bhi aapki premika nhi hai...aur mere paas bhi koi nhi hai...toh hum dono kyu na ek hojaye..." Rani said leaning closer.

" Iss deal se hum dono ka fayda hai..." Rani said.

" Durr hato humse...hum tumhe saza dilakar rahenge..." Anubhav yelled.

" Aree oo Anubhav...teen baar saza de chuka hai kanoon par phir bhi ye bhaag ke aahi gyi..." Genda said.

" Aur hum bhi toh bhaag ke aaye hai...kuch nhi bigad sakti police humar a..." Genda said laughing.

" Itna bada blast plan kiya...kisi ko bhanak bhi nhi lagi...toh iski kaha bhanak lagegi..." Genda spoke.

" Aur tumhari phooti kismat iss baar nhi bachni degi tumhe...waise iss janam mein Haseena toh tumhe milne se rhi...agle janam mein try karlen a...nai toh mai hu hi..." Rani said in wrong way.

" Mar kyu na jaaye par tumse haath milane ka soch bhi nhi sakte...." Anubhav roared.

" Do purane apradhii ka milan hai Anubhav...iss baar nhi bach paoge..." Genda said smirking.

" Khair iss...nazuka ko hosh aane toh do...phir ek saath tum dono ki chutti kardenge...tab tak tum bhi humari deal ke baare mein soch lena..." Rani said leaning closer the last time.

" Ye force abhi tak kyu nhi pohocha...aur pata nhi Shivani aur Amar tak news pohochi bhi hai yaa nhi...unka yaha hona bohot jaruri hai...aakhir woh dono hi gawah ka kaam kar sakte hai.." A tensed Anubhav thought.

———————————

Meanwhile at Chakorgao..

" Headquarters se mail hai...Shivani aur Amar ko Lucknow bulaya hai..." Mihir said viewing a mail from his laptop.

" Abhi nikalna hoga issi wakt...urgent hai..." Mihir said reading the urgency.

" Lagta hai koi lawyer humari case par kaam nhi karna chahta...isiliye aap dono ko bulaya hai...." Mihir said as written in the mail.

" Par waha jake kya karna hai...kaha jaana hai..." Shivani asked.

" Station par aapko Anubhav ka detective mil jayega...wahi le jayega apko..." Mihir said.

" Toh chaliye phir...aakhiri padav bhi par kardenge..." Amar said smiling with confidence.

Author's POV

Shivani and Amar instantly left for Lucknow while other patriots prayed .In span of 5hrs the train stopped at Lucknow junction.

As informed by Mihir,Anubhav's detective took them first to the head-quarters to fulfill every single legal formalities and then to the location from where the detective recieved the signal the extra police force followed them too.______________

" Shivani aur lamba pole kaha gye hai...Amma..." Mithhi asked Karishma.

" Woh bohot jaruri kaam se gye hai...aajayenge thode din mein..." A tensed Karishma said with a smile to Mithii.

" Accha aap ye batao Mithii...aapne ye Amma word kaise sikha...Aap unhe Mumma ya kuch aur bhi keh sakti thi...toh Amma hi kyu..." Haseena asked distracting Mithii from the current tensed situation.

" Maine Papa aur Amma ko suna tha...woh dono Dadi ko Amma keh ke pukarte the...hume woh shabd accha laga aur uska matlab bhi pata chal gya...Toh humne woh hi bol diya..." Mithii smartly explained.

" Waise Mithii aap Shivani ko naam se mat bulaya karo woh badi haina aapse.." Karishma said.

" Mai bolti thi usse pehle Tai...par usne mana kar diya...usne bola ki tu Tai mat bulaya kar mujhe accha nhi lagta...Shivani bolne ko usne hi kaha..." Mithii casually said.

" Agar usse koi poblem nhi hai toh koi baat nhi..." Pushpaji said like Mithii.

" Dadi...poblem nhi problem hota hai wo..." Mithii corrected Pushpaji and everyone chuckled.

" Ekdam..shehad jaisa lagta hai...iske muh se Dadi sunna...." Pushpaji said kissing Mithii.

" Lage kyu na...Aakhir naam joh Mithii hai.." Mihir said pulling her cheeks.

" Par hai bohot teekhi..." Billu whispered but everyone heard.

Mithii angrily glared at Billu.

" Ae tere maa se darrta hu mein..tujhse nhi...aise mat dekh mujhe..." Billu murmured

" Billu mamu..." Mithii got up from her place taking the bottle kept on the side table and ran behind Billu who had already ran away.

Karishma ran after Mithii to stop her while others facepalmed themselves.

Rani's intentions towards Anubhav aren't right!!!

How will Anubhav & Santosh make the criminal duo confess their crime?

Will MPT get justice?

To know keep reading" THE AFTERMATH "

Do vote & comment.

"Remember votes & comments, motivate me to write the next part early "

" Votes & Comments are key to early & interesting updates "

~ Kishaaa

Fight

Ek maaze ki baat hai last mein padhna!!

____

" Santosh utho..." Anubhav tried to wake Santosh who was still unconscious but still no response.

" Aree Anubhav babu...kahe usse pareshaan kar rahe ho.." Genda said entering.

" Waise tumne pucha nhi ki mai ye sab kyu kar rhi hu..." Genda said roaming around the chair.

" Mai hi bata deti hu...woh kya hai na...tum logo ne mujhe arrest kiya...mera itna bada plan fail kardiya...isiliye aur sabse badi wajah...tumhari police ne mere pati ki jaan li..." Genda revealed.

" Aapke pati toh..." Anubhav got confused.

" Aree woh toh bas uss virus ke liye tha...uss Haseena ke chachaji toh bohot bhole hai ussi baat ka faydaa uthaya...Aur mera pati tum police logo ki vajah se maara gaya...ab dekho ek ek police walo se badala lungi..." Genda said in a bad attitude.

" Aisa kuch nhi kar paaogi tum..." Anubhav roared.

" Aree...tum chinta na karo...mai karke dikhaungi na tumhe..." Genda said.

" Bohot kuch karke dikhana hai Anubhav...tumhe bhi toh haasil karna hai..." Rani said entering.

Author's POV

Before Rani could come near Anubhav the door broke with thud.Amar with some extra police forces made an entry to protect the patriots and nation.While Shivani and other officers were out for emergency need.

Anubhav who was worried about the arrival of Amar & Shivani was relie ved.Now he knew MPT will soon get justice.

As Amar entered in the police officers sealed the place not to let the criminal escape.Rani & Genda had no idea that this would happen.Anubhav was a step ahead at everything.

Rani whistling called the goons.And the fight began.It wasn't hard for A well built Amar to knock this untrained goons.

But the duo too had backup.More goons were called!Anubhav sensing the serious situation got up from his chair escaping from hold of threads which had already loosened.

Anubhav grabbed one of the goon from back holding his shoulder.The goon turned to him that's when Anubhav slapped both of his cheeks at a time.So hardly that blood started flowing out from his mouth and he was knocked down then and there.

Amar handled the other one by kicking his stomach and holding one of his leg and spining him on the ground.

Anubhav slapped the next one while Amar slapped his neighbouring on e.Both the goons colliding their heads went unconscious.

Amar and Anubhav shared a victory smile.And again continued the fight.

Anubhav whistled signalling Shivani to enter with other officers.

Shivani entered making the criminal duo widen their eyes looking at the amount of force they had!

Shivani kicked the goon who blocked her way hardly and landed him on the ground.Punching the goon on his nose Shivani knocked the second one.One grabbed Shivani's hairs from back unknown to her.Shivani screamed in pain and back kicked the goon on the part where sun doesn't shine making him yell in pain

During this whole fight Rani & Genda were standing in the corner scared but didn't depict their fear on their face.Rani was double scared then Genda.

Seeing everyone busy in fighting.A goon approached Santosh who was still unconscious due to the high dosage of chloroform. As the goon was about to punch her Santosh held his fist twisting it hardly hand kicked his part with force.Anubhav had already untied her ropes.Santosh too joined the fight.Making the trio sigh a relief.

A goon lifting a chair approached towards Anubhav who's back was facing him.And hardly banged the chair on his back.But to his surprise the chair got in pieces rather than hurting Anubhav's back.The goon realising how strong Anubhav was fainted then and there making Anubhav chuckle.

Soon all the goons were defeated.

And the team was closer to their victory.-

Tried to write a fighting sequence for the first time!!How was the feel?

How will be the proofs displayed in the court??

How will the duo react on the news of MPT members being alive?

How does Shivani know Rani already?

To know keep reading" THE AFTERMATH "

Do vote & comment.

"Remember votes & comments, motivate me to write the next part early "

" Votes & Comments are key to early & interesting updates "

~ Kishaaa

Just noticed it after reading the previous part!!!Writer ne khud Anubhav ko Haseena ka bhai bana diya!!! Mujhe laga koi notice karega toh maza aayega isiliye jaan bhuj ke correct nhi kiya

Bye

Victory

A uthor's POV

The scene in godown was vice verse now.Having no option Rani and Genda had too surrender now.They were tied to the chairs with ropes same as Anubhav and Santosh were tied by them

The commissioner of Lucknow was arriving at the location to record the statement by himself.________

" Shivani ek baar mujhe uss se milne doh..." Rani started pleading Shivani.

" Kiske baare mein baat kar rhi hai ye...aur aap kaise jaanti hai isse..." Anubhav asked confused.

" Shivani please ek baar mujhe meri beti se mila do..." Shivani fake cried.

" Iski beti bhi hai..." Santosh asked Shivani.

" Ha hai..." Shivani said.

" Aur tum kisse milne ki baat kar rhi ho...wahi beti na jise tumne chod diya...bas 2 saal ki thi wo tab...tab kaha gayi thi tumhari akal..." Shivani asked in anger.

" Maaf karo mujhe...par ab mujhe milna hai usse...mai apni galti manti hu... Mujhe milwa doh usse..." Rani pleaded joining her hands.

" Jitna in sab logo me tumhare baare mein bataya hai na...mujhe nhi lagta tum sudhar sakti ho... ye bass natak hai tumhara saza se bachne ka..." Shivani said the truth.

" Kaha hai wo...kesi hai..woh toh batado..." Rani again pleaded

" Ye toh nhi bata sakti wo kaha hai...par jaha hai waha bohot khush hai.. .tumhari buri nazar uss tak pohochne bhi nhi dungi..." Shivani spoke for the last time.

" Commissioner sir aagaye hai..." Anubhav said.

Author's POV

The police siren echoed in the godown turning Rani and Genda pale while Anubhav Santosh Amar Shivani smiled proudly.

The commissioner entered with a proud smile.________

" I am proud of you team..." The commisioner said and the team smiled back.

" Recording start karo..." The commissioner ordered and approached towards Rani & Genda.

" Pehli baat bol raha hu...khud apne kiye hue gunaah qubool karlo...dusri baar haath bolega..." Commissioner threated the duo.

Author's POV

One by one Rani and Genda confessed all their crimes.Rani and Genda had teamed up in the jail.Genda had contributed in this blast only to take a revenge of her husbands death which was due to the crime he had done!!Her husband's case was looked by the MPT members unknown to them who he was!!

Rani also had a similar reason as Haseena had punished her lover to death because of the crime done by him.Rani also confessed about her prior crimes right from Fake Haseena to her last case led by Naina Mathur.Rani accepted that she has mislead Shivani about her health and hand overed her daughter.

At last the constable took them to their home of course IB jail as they weren't any nominal criminals now!!They will be hanged to death after completing the formalities.

Shivani and Amar signed the proof papers as the whole scenario was watched by them.

Finally the MPT had got justice!!!Now the only work left was rebuilding the MPT and handing it over to the patriots.___________

As the criminal duo was arrested Amar Shivani Santosh Anubhav shared a group hug.

" Anubhav...maine bhi toh madat ki hai..." The commission urf Anubhav's bestfriend complained.

Anubhav took him into the hug instantly.

" Ab lagte hai mahila police thane ke kaam pein..." The commissioner said smiling.

"Jarur..." Anubhav said in enthusiasm.

" Commissioner sir please mera transfer phir se MPT mein kara dijiye..." Santosh whinned.

" Try jarur karunga..." The commissioner said with a smile.

" Bass ab thane ke asli hakdaaro ko ye baat bata do...." Commissioner said keeping a hand Anubhav's shoulder.

" Ji...hum nikalenge abhi..." Anubhav smiled.

" Mai rebuilding ke orders de deta hu..." Commisioner sir said.__________

Boarding the train the saviours began their journey towards Chakorgao controlling the happiness of their victory.

" Kitne khush honge na sab..." Shivani said smiling.

" Bohot khush hojayenge..." Anubhav said.

" Anu bhaiyaa...aapko kuch bhi karke madam sir patana hai...mujhe phir cyber cell nhi jaana...mai kaam karungi toh MPT mein hi..." Santosh ordered.

" Thik hai karlenge baat..." Anubhav said pulling her cheek.

" Waise aap dono thik haina...koi chot wagaira nhi hai na..." Amar asked and Anubhav and Santosh exchange glances.

" Nhi hum bilkul thik hai..." Anubhav faked.

" Mai bhi thik hu..." Santosh too.

" Waise aap dono ke liye kuch hai surprise jaisa..." Shivani said.

" Humare liye...surprise.." Santosh and Anubhav questioned.

" Ha...chal ke pata chal jayega..." Amar said.________________

Author's POV

Here in Chakorgao no one had an idea of their arrival.

On reaching Pawar Vada,Amar and Shivani rang the bell while Anubhav and Santosh hid themselves.Cheetah opened the door and fear rised up. Amar and Shivani were standing with a pale and sad face at the door._____

———

" Kya hua...aap log aise kyu muh latakaye hai..." Cheetah fearfully asked.

" Woh..." Shivani pretended to be sad.

" Woh...kya..Sab thik hai na..." Cheetah said making everybody gather at the door.

" Jiji...Aise muh kahe latkai ho..." Binni asked confusingly.

" Ha boliye kya hua...Aur aap dono akele kaise wapas aaye...Anubhav aur Santu kaha hai..." Haseena asked.

" Woh..." Amar pretended now.

" Woh kya..." Pushpaji asked.

" Surprise !!!!..." Anubhav and Santosh jumped from either side of door making everyone gasp.

" Anu bhaiyaa...santu..." Karishma said in shock.

" Ye kya mazak tha...." Haseena said keeping her hands on her waist.

" Pata hai kitna dar gye the hum sab...." Mihir said in a angry tune.

" Aree shaant hojaiye...hum aagaye na..." Santosh said.

" Ab andar aaye...ya yhi..." Anubhav said as they had covered the entrance.

Everyone cleared the entrance and they got in.

" Case solve hogaya..." Anubhav exclaimed in happiness.

Happiness now had no bounds.Everyone hugged each other and shed few tears of happiness.

" Kaun hai..." Mithii who was sleeping on the sofa itself got up hearing the happiness.

Everybody who turned hearing Mithii.While Santosh and Anubhav were questioningly looking at Mithii.

" Ye kaun hai..." Anubhav questioned while Mithii scanned him from top to bottom.

" Aur ek lamba pole..." Mithii said standing on floor and looking at Anubhav lifting her neck upwards.

Everyone chuckled at her statement.

" Lamba pole...??" Anubhav & Santosh said.

" Aap pehle baithiye toh...hum batate hai sabkuch..." Pushpaji said.

" Aate hi panchayat shuru..." Billu murmured.

Anubhav and Santosh got seated waiting for everyone to start the conversation.

" Ab bataiye kaun hai ye bacchi..." Santosh asked.

" Bacchi nhi...Mithii hu mai.." Mithii grumpily corrected Santosh.

" Ha ye Mithii hai..." Karishma said.

"Aage...?" Anubhav questioned.

" Ye aap dono ki bhanji hai..." Mihir revealed.

" Kya.. " Anubhav & Santosh exclaimed with mixed emotions.

" Ha humne aur Karu ne isse god lene ka phaisla kiya hai..." Mihir said.

" Mithii...ye dekho ye tumhare mama aur maasi..." Karishma introduced.

" Ohh!! Toh ye lamba pol mere mama hai...aur ye maasi..." Mithii said

" Lamba pole kya hota hai..." Anubhav questioned

" Aap ye....itne lambe ho dono...isse lamba pole kehte hai..." Mithii said lifting her hand up.

" Mithii chalo tum sone...raat hogayi hai bohot..." Karishma said taking Mithii to room.

" Ab pata chala ye tha surprise..." Shivani smilingly said.

" Par ye hua kaise..." Anubhav asked and Mihishma narrated.

" Mujhe tum sabko kuch batana hai..." Shivani said in a serious tone.

" Kya..." Haseena questioned.

" Mithii ki maa Rani hai..." Shivani revealed a shocking news.

" Ye tum kya keh rhi ho..." Karishma said in shivering voice.

" Ha..sach hai ye...mai nhi janti thi ki Rani kaun hai...par aaj usse dekhne ke baad pata chala...usne mujhse joh bola 8 saal pehle wo sab jhoot tha...." Shivani said.

" Abhi usse god lene ka faisala tum par hai..." Shivani said looking Mihishma.

" Ra...Rani ka kya hua...?" Karishma asked.

" Genda aur Rani dono ko faansi hogi kuch dino mein..." Anubhav quietly said.

There was a pin drop silence in the room.Everyone were still digesting the fact that Mithii was Rani a criminals daughter.

" Hum humara faisala nhi badlenge..." Karishma spoke.

" Hogi Mithii Rani ki beti par...par wo uske jaisi bilkul nhi hai...hum usse acche sanskaar denge..." Karishma emotionally said.

" Hum adhure hai Mithii ke bina...humara faisala whi hai..." Mihir too announced and everyone proudly looked towards Mihishma.

" Mujhe tum dono se yhi umeed thi..." Shivani said.

" Par ye blast kiya kyu tha unn dono ne..." Cheetah asked.

" Woh ...." Anubhav & Santosh narrated all the happenings.

" Dhanyavaad Shivji...." Pushpaji said praying.

" Aur humara thana..." Karishma emotionally asked.

" Rebuilding ke liye orders de diye...kuch mahino mein humare hawaale hoga..." Santosh said.

" Thank you Shivani...agar tum uss waqt hume nhi bachati toh...na hi hum zinda hote na hume insaaf milta..." Haseena thanked Shivani.

" Kya re jazbaat wali bai...mein bhi toh hissa hu na iss parivaar ka mujhe thank you mat bol..." Shivani said a bit emotionally.

" Ant Bhala toh sab bhala...." Binni said.

" Ab madam sir...hum nhi manne wale...jab tak humara thana ban raha hai...tabtak Anubhav sir aur aapki shaadi hogi..." Pushpaji announced.

" Par..." Anuseena were about to speak.

" Humne keh diya matlab keh diya...." Pushpaji said.

" Wohooo...." Everyone exclaimed motivating Anuseena.

" Thik hai hum taiyaar hai..." Anuseena agreed.

" Sirf inn dono ki nai aur kisi bhi shaadi hogi...." Mithii gave a surprise entry.

" Tum jagi hui ho..." Karishma asked.

" Ha toh tum kitna gondhal kar rha the..." Mithii said again messing up the language.

" Hum dono ready nhi hai...Shaadi je liye...kyu cheete..." Santosh escaped and Cheetah agreed.

" Tum dono ki nhi re..." Mithii said going towards Shivani and raising her heartbeats.

" Inn dono ki..." Mithii said keeping Amar & Shivani's hand in each other and everyone made a ' O ' face.

" Tum logo ko pata nhi hai...inn dono ka chakkar chal raha hai...Amma shapath...Pucho inse..." Mithii said making everyone widen there eyes with her talks.

" Ye Sach mein 8 saal ki hi haina..." Billu wondered.

" Jiji...ye sach ke rhi hai..." Binni said looking at Shivani.

" Ye...ha...mai batane wali thi..." Shivani tried to speak.

" Matlab sach hai...??" Binni questioned.

" Ha...." Shivani finally revealed.

'" Ohh lambe pol.... aap bhi bolo sach hai..." Mithii said scaring Amar.

" Ha ye sach hai..." Amar too confessed.

" Amar...aapki gaadi toh bohot aage nikal gyi..." Anubhav teased his friend.

" Toh tai raha...Inn bhi shaadi hogi.." Pushpaji exclaimed.

" Kaha tha na mat bata...ab ja nhi deti tujhe kairiya..." Shivani said pulling Mithii ear.

" Aa..h...Amma..." Mithii said rubbing her ears in pain.

" Mat de...meri Amma hai na woh degi mujhe kairi..." Mithii said teasing her with a tongue out.

Victory is with MPT

Finally the culprits are caught!!

And many things are revealed!!

Also wedding bells are ringing

Keep reading" THE AFTERMATH "

Do vote & comment.

"Remember votes & comments, motivate me to write the next part early "

" Votes & Comments are key to early & interesting updates "

~ Kishaaa

Grateful

□ 07-03-2024

One more achievement...The story got 9th position in top 10 in India.

Unfortunately I don't have any screenshot nor i have seen it!!

But a huge thanks to my readers who informed me with the same excitement as i would!!!

Grateful for your love.Keep supporting ❤

~ Kishaaa ❤.

Care

Having their dinner everyone departed to their rooms.

" Cheete kya hua tu aise kyu dekh raha mujhe..." Santosh irritatedly said to Cheetah as he was worriedly staring at her from a long time.

" Santuji...aapko sach mein koi chot nhi hai na...hume kyu lag raha hai ki aap jhooth bol rhi hai..." Cheetah suspiciously asked.

" Nai...cheete mai sach mein...thik hu...." Santosh again lied.

" Toh..." Cheetah said and pulled her over his chest holding her wrist.

" Aaah...chod cheete kya kar rha hai..." Santosh whined in pain as her wrist hurted.

" Sorry...Santuji...bas wo tarika tha..." Cheetah said separating themselves.

" Bataya kyu nhi santuji...aapko dard hai..." Cheetah said examining her sprained wrist.

" Mai tujhe pareshaan nhi karna chahti thi..." Santosh said with teary eyes.

" Kahe ka pareshaan yaha aapka haath sujh gaya hai...aapko kitna takleef hua hoga humne aisa kheecha toh..." Cheetah said in guilt.

" Baithiye idhar...hum spray laate hai..." Cheetah said making her sit on bed.

" Laaiye haath..." Cheetah said and Santosh forwarded her hand.

" Hum ye bilkul accha nahi laga santuji...aap aise chupaya mat kijiye humse apna dard..." Cheetah said sadly.

" Aree cheete muh kyu latkaya tune...mai pakka tujhe bataungi aage se..." Santosh said lifting his mood up.

" Ab sojaiye...Aur aap aaj bed pe sojaiye..." Cheetah said.

Though Cheetosh were living in a single room.Cheetah didn't wanted to make Santosh uncomfortable.Hence they were sleeping separately.Green Forest...

" Nai cheeta tu bhi bed pein soja na...please..." Santosh insisted.

" Par..." Cheetah refused

" Mai tere saath bohot comfortable hu...aana cheete mujhe tere paas sona hai..." Santosh pleaded with puppy eyes.

Taking his blanket Cheetah got on bed.

" Good Night..." Santosh wished looking at his face.

" Good Night " Cheetah nervously wished back.______________

Meanwhile,

Author's POV

As Anuseena got into their room,Haseena hugged Anubhav tightly.

Anubhav got a slight pain in his back arm but he knew Haseena needed this.He too hugged her back and patted her back to calm her.___________

" Aap thik haina Anu...." Haseena asked still resting her head on his chest.

" Hum bilkul thik hai...aap hi ke samaksh hai..." Anubhav said.

" Humne aapko bohot miss kiya..." Haseena softly said.

" Humne bhi..." Anubhav said keeping his chin on her head.

" Par hum aapse gussa hai..." Haseena said instantly sat on bed.

" Aree kya hua...abhi gale laga liya aur ekdam se durr bhaag gyi..." Anubhav said getting beside her.

" Aur nhi toh kya...aate hi kya aapne dara diya...Amar aur Shivani dono ko aage bhej kar...wo sadi hui shakal lekar...pata hai hum kitna darr gye the...." Haseena grumpily said.

" Woh toh bas mazaak tha priyeee....hum itne dino baad itne khush the....toh socha mazaak karlein..." Anubhav said.

" Par hum kitna darr gye the....kitne bure khyaal aarahe the humare dimag mein...." A teary Haseena said.

" Haseenaji...aapko pata hai hume aapke aankhon mein aansu nhi acche lagte....kyu ro rhi hai...hum thik hai..." Anubhav said cupping her face.

" Hum nhi reh sakte aapke bina...isiliye darr lagta hai hume..." Haseena said again taking him into a hug.

" Ab hum aapka vachan dete hai...phir aisa mazaak bilkul nhi karenge...bass aap humse naraaz nhi hona..." Anubhav said and Haseena breaking the hug looked at him.

" Pinky promise..." Haseena said forwarding her little finger for promise.

" Gulabi vachan..." Anubhav said making Haseena laugh at his words.

" Kuch bhi hindi bolte hai aap...kabhi kabhi..." Haseena said and both lied down on bed.

" Anu...sojaiye na..." Haseena irritedly said in between her sleep as Anubhav was continusly tossing in sleep.

" Hmmm..." Anubhav hummed.

" Ek min...aap uthiye...aur shirt utariye..." Haseena boldly said.

" Haseenaji...aap ye kya bol rhi hai..." Anubhav jumped and sat on the bed hearing her order.

" Joh kaha hai wo kariye..." Haseena said switching the light on.

" Hume pata hai...aapko chot lagi hai...aap bata nhi rahe hai...ab dekhiye hum aapse baat hi nhi karenge..." Haseena angrily said.

" Pri..." Anubhav was about to say but..

" Humne kaha voh kariye..." Haseena said still in an angry tone taking the first aid box in hand and coming to him.

" Thik hai..." Anubhav got scared from his to be wife and nervously started undoing his t-shirt.

" Aap itni bold hai...pata nhi tha hume..." Anubhav tried to change the situation.

" Bold..ab koi hindi shabd nhi yaad aaraha...joh kaha hai wo kariye..." Haseena taunted.

Making Haseena widen her eyes seeing the wound Anubhav removed his tshirt closing his eyes and getting ready to face her taunts.

" Anubhav...ye itni badi chot hai...aur aap keh rahe aap thik hai...ye toh accha hai ki hum samaj gye...nai toh infection hojata..." Haseena scolded.

" Lagta hai aapko IB ki training mein ye sab nhi batate...tabhi toh aap aisi harkate karte hai..." Haseena again scolded.

" Kaisi lagi ye goli..." Haseena asked.

" Goli nhi..." Anubhav was about to speak but..

" Accha...matlab IB mein jhoot bolna sikhate hai...par chot ko thik karna nhi sikhaate...Hum bhi police mein hai...acche se pata hai ye kiska ghaav hai..." Haseena again showered him with her taunts.

" Sorry...wo Rani ko pakadte wakt..." Anubhav said still scared.

" Rani ne goli chalayi aap par..." Haseena's anger had no bounds.

" Aap kyu krodh kar rhi hai...shaant hojaiye..." Anubhav dared to speak.

" Mudiye udhar...karne diniye first aid..." Haseena said not so sweetly.

" Pura bandage khul chuka hai...phir bhi batana nhi janab ko..." Haseena angrily murmured.

" Maafi chate hai...ab bataiyenge aapko agli baar se..." Anubhav said but Haseena was busy cleaning the wound.

" Ek toh pehle se chot ki vajah se dard hai...ab dil bhi dard kar raha hai...a apko krodhit dekhkar..." Anubhav expressed his situation.

" Accha aapko dard bhi hota hai...hume pata hi nhi tha..." Haseena again taunted with an extra sweet smile.

Readers be like :- " Taano ki barsaat nikli aage...Haseenaji ke dwaare..."

" Dhiree...." Anubhav whinned as Haseena mistakenly pressured her hand.

" Sorry sorry...." Haseena now softly said.

" Aap ro rhi hai..." Anubhav asked as drop fell on his shoulder.

" Toh...ro nhi toh kya kare...aap dhyaan kyu nhi rakhte khud ka..." Haseena tearfully said.

" Kyunki aap haina..." Anubhav said taking her hand in his as the first aid was done.

" Promise kariye... " Haseena forwaded her pinky finger.

" Promise..." Anubhav promised.

Claming the Haseena's anger and pain of both the couple dozed off to sleep in each other arms.

Tried my best writing Cheetosh moments!!!

How was taano ki barsaat?

Shivmar & Mihishma fans don't get upset!!!Something's on the way!!

Keep reading" THE AFTERMATH "

Do vote & comment.

"Remember votes & comments, motivate me to write the next part early "

" Votes & Comments are key to early & interesting updates "

~ Kishaaa

Happiness

Author's POV

A new day began after a peaceful night.Months after everyone had a very peaceful sleep.No tension,no thinking nothing just mind at peace.

The sunrise radiated a positive vibe.Chakorgao as always was sparkling with greenery of nature and the river flowing melodiously.

Pawar Vada was still asleep may be because of the happiness they received the day before.

At Mihishma's room,little Mithii was soundly sleeping between her pare nts.While Mihishma protecting her from sides.As the morning rays fell on Karishma's closed eyes her sleep got disturbed.Karishma getting up pulled the curtains on not allowing the rays disturb her dear husband's and lovely daughter's sleep.

Karishma layed on her place carressing Mithii's hairs and a peaceful smile captured her face.

Mihir coming out of his slumber opened his eyes noticing the most beautiful ladies in front them.Mihishma's eyes met and they smiled at each other._________

" Aise kyu muskura rahe hai..." Karishma spoke in low voice.

" Tumhe muskurata dekh kar apne aap muskan aajati hai...." Mihir said still smiling.

" Khush hai na aap..." Karishma asked don't why!!

"Khushi ki itni vajah hote hue koi kaise dukhi reh sakta hai...." Mihir said intervening his hands with hers.

" Humne thik faisala liya na...Mithii ko apna ke..." Karishma asked in a low voice.

" Ha karu...sabse sahi faisala hai ye humara..." Mihir said.

" Iski taraf dekho...ye bhi toh pyaar deserve karti hai...aur hum wahi kar rahe hai..." Mihir said adoring Mithii.

" Hmm...isne khud ke saath saath humare bhi ghaav bhar diye..." Karishma said kissing Mithii's forehead.

" Humare liye ye kisi farishte se kam nhi hai Mithii.." Mihir said still adoring her.

Mihishma kissed either sides of Mithii cheek slightly not disturbing her sleep.

" Hume kairii khani hai..." Mithii murmured in sleep making Mihishma giggle.

" Amma..." Mithii snuggled into Karishma and again slept.

" Ye jab hume Amma bolti haina...bohot alag ehsaas hota hai...shayad wahi.." Karishma said thinking about her baby who was no more.

" Karu...mat taaze karo unn ghau ko...mai janta hu...bhulna aasaan nhi hai...par tumhe ye karna hoga..." Mihir encouraged and Karishma agreed.

" Amma..." Mithii murmured.

" Hum yhi hai Mithii..." Karishma replied.

" Papa..." Mithii next murmured.

" Hum bhi yhi hai..." Mihir replied caressing her back.

" Uthana nhi hai aapko..." Karishma asked Mithii who was still snnugled into her.

" Pata nhi...mujhe bohot nind aarahi hai aaj..." Mithii said.

" Accha..toh koi baat nhi...sojao..." Karishma said tapping her back to sleep.

" Tum dono bhi chalo na...aaj mere saath mandir...mujhe tum dono ko milana hai bappa se..." Mithii said turning on her back and slightly opening her eyes.

" Hum bhi chale..." Karishma thought looking at Mihir.

" Ha...bilkul hum bhi chalenge...aaj hum teeno jayenge..." Mihir said and Mithii kissed his cheek smiling.

" Ab nhj sona aapko..." Karishma said settling Mithii's messed up hairs.

" Nai...abhi hum teeno mandir jayenge...chalo utho nahalo..." Mithii ordered.

" Aur ha...pilla kuch pehena...bappa ko accha lagega..." Mithii cutely said.

" Accha thik hai..." Karishma said cupping her face.___________

" Aap dono itna taiyaar hue hai...kuch hai kya aaj..." Haseena wondered looking at Mihishma who were dressed.

" Ha hum bhi vahi soch raje hai..." Pushpaji said.

" Lagta hai...aap dono ki anniversary hai...Happy Anniversary" Santosh cheerfully wished.

" Aree nhi...sab sab jadbuddhi hai...nai hai humara anniversary aaj..." Karishma clear the false news as every began wishing her.

" Kya Amma...aap bhi..." Mihir said looking at Pushpaji in disbelief.

" Ha..wo..behek gye...yaad tha hume..." Pushpaji dramatically said.

" Kaha jaa rahe hai aap itni subah subah..." Billu asked.

" Hum tino jaa rahe hai...bappa ke mandir..." Mithii said getting into the conversation.

" Waise Binni Shivani Amar sir kaha hai..." Karishma asked.

" Woh Binni ke gaav mein kuch problem hui toh usse bula liya...Shivani aur Amar usse hi chodne gyi hai station..." Haseena replied.

" Aur madam sir...Anu bhaiya...woh kaha hai uthe nhi ab tak..." Karishma surprisingly asked.

" Aapke bhai ko goli lagi thi mission par...dawai ke asar ki vajah se abhi tak so rahe hai..." Haseena replied in not so normal way.

" Check up toh karliya hai na...infection vagera..." Mihir asked.

" Ha..ha..lucknow mein treatment ho gyi hai...ek baar aap chahe toh dekh lena..." Haseena replied.

" Ha...aake dekhte hai..." Mihir replied.

" Shivani ko bata dena..." Karishma said leaving.

" Aree...Amma maine bata diya hai use subah...baar baar bolne ko wo koi teacher nhi hai...Abhi chalo.." Mithii irritatedly said as Karishma was taking time to leave while others chuckled.

" Ha maate aarahe hai..." Karishma exited.___________

" Aree...Mithii...aaj der kardi..." The panditji asked Mithii.

" Ha..hogayii der...par mein aaj kisi ke saath aayi hu..." Mithii cheerfully said.

" Kiske saath...roj toh akelu bhatakti rehti hai yaha waha... " Panditji asked.

" Inse milo...mere Amma Papa..." Mithii said holding Mihishma's hands.

" Namaskar..." Panditji stood up at respect greeting Mihishma.

" Namaste..." Mihishma greeted back.

" Aap...Amma...papa..." Panditji confusedly asked.

" Ha...humne Mithii ko god liya hai..." Mihir politely said.

" Accha...Bohot acchu jodi hai aapki...shakshat shankar parvati..." Panditji said adoring the couple.

" Aaiye...aarti kariye aap teeno..." Panditji gestured.

Worshipping Lord Ganesha the family felt peace.

" Bagitlas Bappa...Mere bhi Mummy Papa hai...aapki tarah..." Mithii said happily praying.

" Ye lijiye prasaad..." Panditji gave them the prasaad.

" Aaj modak..." Mithii surprisingly said.

" Lagta hai...tere bappa ko pata tha...ki tu aaj tere parivaar ke saath aayegi ...isiliye modak hai..." Panditji said.

" Hmmm...mere bappa hai..sab pata toh hoga hi..." Mithii proudly said._

" Aashram kyu jaana hai..." Mithii asked Mihishma as they walked towards the orphanage.

" Kyuki tum ab se humare saath rahogi...isske liye kuch thodi bohot taiyaari hoti hai...wo karni hai...." Mihir explained.

" Tum aapne doste se bhi mil lo..." Karishma said.

" Dost...mera yaha koi dost nhi hai...mujhe nhi milna kisi se..." Mithii grumpily expressed.

" Accha mat milna...kaam toh pura karle...Shivani bhi aarahi hai..." Karishma said.

" Aap yaha baith jaiye mein madam ko bulati hu..." One of the lady in the orphanage said while Mithii gave her a bombastic side eye.

" Aaye nhi madam..." Shivani said entering.

" Nai..wo kabhi time pein aayi toh na..humesha aapna sada hua muh lekar der se aati hai..." Mithii said.

" Ae...dhire bol sun legi toh gadbad hojayegi..." Shivani stopped Mithii.

Mithii quickly shifted over Karishma's lap making weird faces looking at the glass door where her enemy Pintyaa who she always complained of stood.

" Dekha ab mujhe mere mummy papa mil gye...mai jaa rhi hu unke saat h...ab khaate reh bina aachar ka khana..." Mithii said going towards him while Pintyaa angrily stormed off making Mihishma giggle.

" Accha sabak mila isse..." Mithii said coming and again settling herself on Karishma's lap proudly.

" Aagayii aap..." Shivani stood as the head arrived.

" Ha aaj thoda late hua...sorry aaiye cabin mein..." The gestured her towards her cabin

" Aaj nhi roz late hoti hai ye...aur yhi bahana martii hai..." Mithii murmured.

" Aap Mithii ko sach mein god lena chahte hai..." The head asked.

" Ha..isiliye yaha aaye hai..." Karishma said.

" Bohot shaitaan hai...naak mein dam karke rakhti hai...pehle ki warning de rhi hu..." The head rudely warned.

" Aapko kya problem hai...waise bhi aap toh chahti thi na...mai yaha se jau...toh ja rahi hu..." Mithii defended herself while Shivani And Mihishma were embrassed.

" Dekha kitni muh fatt hai..." The head said looking at Mithii.

" Ji aap kaam ki baat karengii toh behtar hai...Hum dekh lenge humari beti kaisi hai....adoption ke papers dijiye..." Mihir defended his daughter.

Shivani & Mihishma continued the procedure while Mithii continued glaring badly at the head.

As the process got over, Mithii holding Mihishma's hands turned back and again pulled out her tongue teasing the head proudly.

A Mihishma part finally with Mithii's touch!!

Hope you all liked it!!!

Keep reading" THE AFTERMATH "

Do vote & comment.

"Remember votes & comments, motivate me to write the next part early "

" Votes & Comments are key to early & interesting updates "

~ Kishaaa

Mother's Love

Next parts may be delayed as i am packed with my college work!!I'll try to update soon

Author's POV

Anubhav Amar and Santosh were off to Lucknow to complete the remaining formalities regarding the case.Moreover Anubhav had planned something special something wanted._________

" Abhi toh hogayi formalities ab kya..." Santosh said.

" Ab kuch hai...chaliye humare saath..." Anubhav said and Amar & Santosh followed him.

" Kaha jarahe hai hum..." Amar asked.

" Shanti rakhiye..." Anubhav calmly said to his friend.

" Hum madam sir ke uncle ke ghar jaa rahe hai..." Santosh guessed the road.

" Ji...hum aaj Maa aur Ammi ko le jarahe hai Chakorgao..." Anubhav smilingly said.

" Madam sir ko batati hu abhi...wo bohot khush hongi...." Santosh said pulled her phone from pocket.

" Rukiye Santosh...hume haseenaji ko ashryachakit karna chahte hai...mat bataiye..." Anubhav stopped.

" Ashcharya...kya bola aapne..." Santosh confusedly asked about tne word.

" Ashcharyachakit...matlab surprise dena hai unhe...." Amar explained and Santosh made a ' O ' face._____________

" Koi nai hai kya ghar pein..." Santosh said as nobody answered the bell.

" Koi nai hota toh taala hota...andar se lock hai darwaza..." Amar said.

Again banging the door Ammi opened.

" Kaun hai bhai....Kabse bajaye jaraha hai..." Ammi said opening the door.

" Tum log...Devkiii..." Ammi called Anubhav's mom seeing the wanted faces.

As Anubhav's mom saw him.She tightly hugged his son.The son she thought would never return was before her fit n fine.Ammi too had tears in her eyes.

" Tu thik hai na beta...kaha tha tu...yaad nhi aati apni maa ki..." Maa said caressing his face.

" Hum bilkul thik hai maa..." Anubhav said holding her hands.

" Kya thik hai...dekh kitna patala hua hai..." Maa said seeing him from head to toes.

" Andar toh le chaliye maa...kabse yhi khade hai..." Anubhav complained cutely.

" Tum..." Ammi tried to recognize Amar.

" Amar Vidrohi..." Amar said politely with a smile.

" Bohot accha ladka hai...Anu ke saath hai bohot saalo se..." Maa praised Amar.

" Tu aise muh kyu latkayi hai..." Ammi questioned Santosh.

" Jabse aaye hai....tabse dekh rahe hai...Aap inn dono se hi baat kar rhi hai...Aap bhul gyi kya muje.." Santosh grumpily said.

" Aree aisa kuch nhi hai...tuj jaisi pyaari bacchi ko koi bhul sakta hai..." Ammi said embracing Santosh.

" Anubhav...Haseena Karishma kaha hai..." Maa tensedly asked.

" Woh maa ammi hume aapko kuch batana hai..." Anubhav seriously said.

" Kya aur tu itna pareshan kyu hogaya..." Maa questioned

" Par promise kijiye aap dono....jyada hyper nhi hongi..." Santosh asked for a promise.

" Kya baat hai Anubhav kuch..." Ammi got scared.

Author's POV

Calming Ammi & Maa and making them ready to face the situation that was going depicted the trio narrated the whole story from the blast to the saving to the criminals and finally to the success.Ammi & Maa were shocked hearing this but calmed themselves not harming their health.And knowing that all of them were healthy & fine now relaxed their racing hea rts.The only thing the duo wanted was to see their kids.Maa was shattered hearing about the loss of Mihishma's baby but the happy news of Mithii relaxed her a little.

Packing their luggage & informing Mahipal uncle who was with Mansi out of town for Mansi's competition they started their journey off to Chakorgao.

Within a span of time they reached the happy place.Ammi & Maa were delighted seeing the atmosphere of Chakorgao.An instant positive energy entered their hearts making then glow freshly.___________

" Itni durr...par jagah bohot acchi hai..." Maa said looking around as they stood at the door of Pawar Vada.

" Ha...ekdum taazi hawa..aaj kaha milti hai ye..." Ammi agreed.

Anubhav rang the bell to which Cheetah opened the door.He was emotional seeing them all he could do was hug Ammi who was a mother figure to him.Cheetah greeted Maa and everyone entered.

" Aap dono...." Pushpaji exclaimed in joy.

" Ha hume hi aana pada...aap toh kuch batati nhi hai..." Maa scolded.

" Chodiye na...ab toh gale lagiye..." Pushpaji hugged Maa & Ammi.

" Maa aur Aap Haseena ki Ammi na..." Mihir said touching their feet.

" Tu toh yaha aagaya...hume nhi bata sakta tha...jaan nikli jaa rhi thi hum ari..." Maa scolded him.

" Batana toh chahte the...par aapki tabiyat ko kharab nhi karsakte the..." Mihir calmly stated.

" Tum Shivani na...bohot bohot shukriyaa...tum nhi hoti toh..." Ammi emotionally said carresing Shivani's cheek.

" Aap mujhe apna maanti haina toh shukriya mat kahiye..." Shivani said with a smile.

" Phir bhi apni jaan par khelkar koi nhi bacha taa kisiko...jitna shukriya kare utna kam hai...." Maa said looking towards Shivani with respect.

" Inn logo ne mere liye bohot kuch jhela hai...inhe bacha na mera farz tha...pariwar se kam nhi hai ye log mere liye..." Shivani said looking at everyone.

" Karu kaha hai..." Maa said looking around.

" Woh uss toofan ko sula rhi hai..." Billu popped.

" Tufaan..." Maa confusedly asked.

" Haa...aapki poti...bilkul aapki beti jaisi hai...bhari hui bandook..." Billu described Mithii.

" Humare saamne humari beti ki poti ki burai kar rahs ho...." Maa fakely scolded Billu.

" Sorry..." Billu felt it a true scolding.

" Aree mazak kar rhe the....tum toh humare bete jaise ho..." Maa said softly.

" Mere dil ka tukda...Haseena kaha hai..." Ammi said as she couldn't find her.

" Chaliye hum le chalte hai aapko..." Anubhav & Mihir said.

Author's POV

As Anubhav took Ammi to Haseena's room her heart felt peace.Her dear daughter was soundly sleeping with her mouth open as always.Ammi walked in and Anubhav left to give them some privacy.

Ammi sat beside Haseena and carressed her hairs tears forming their place in her eyes.Haseena smiled in her slumber as she felt a motherly touch .Ammi kissed her forehead which made Haseena open her eyes.Haseena looked at Ammi and chuckled and turned to another side again sleeping

.___________

" Ammi bhi na...humesha sapne mein hi aati hai..." Haseena murmured in sleep which depicted how badly she missed her Ammi.

" Hasuu...dekh mein tere saamne hu...nhi milegi mujse..." Ammi said caressing her hair.

" Ammi..." Haseena said turning back to Ammi.

" Ha dekh mein milne aayi hu..." Ammi said cupping her face.

A teary Haseena was in Ammi's lap hugging her tightly and hiding her face in her stomach feeling peace.

" Shaant hoja Hassu..." Ammi tried calming her as Haseena broke seeing her Ammi.

" Humne bohot miss kiya aapko..." Haseena said in between hiccups.

" Ab nhi jaane dungi tujhe durr..." Ammi said kissing her forehead.

" Tu thik hai na..." Ammi asked and Haseena nodded.

" Maa...woh bhi aayi hai..." Haseena asked.

" Ha...woh karishma se milne gyi hai..." Ammi told.

Haseena making herself comfortable with her Ammi soon slept hugging her mom like a little baby!!!

Meanwhile at Mihishma's room.

Author's POV

Karishma was patting Mithii to sleep who had hided her face in Karishma comforting embrace.The whole scene was lovingly adored by Maa which made her a little emotional.Mihir left as to give them privacy as Maa entered the room.___________

"Karu...." Maa lovingly called her daughter.

Karishma turned as soon as she heard her mom's voice.

" Maa..." Karishma got up seeing her mother.

" Kaisii hai tu..." Maa asked knowing the answer.

" Thik hai hum..." Karishma faked.

" Apni maa se jhut bolegii..." Maa emotionally said.

Karishma hugged mom tightly venting out all her emotions which would come out in Maa's presence only!!

" Bohot galat hua hai....par hum ussi ko toh mann mein liye nhi beth sakte na Karu..." Maa said carresing her back calming her down.

" Tu dekhna bhagwaan ne tere liye kitna pyaara farishta bheja hai..." Maa said looking at Mithii who was soundly sleeping.

" Wahi toh hai humari jeene ki vajah...humari pyaari Mithii..." Karishma said adoring Mithii still hugging her mom.

" Aapko koi problem nhi haina..." Karishma askef regarding Mithii.

" Bhala mujhe kyu problem hogi...mujhe meri poti mil gyi...mai khush hu..." Maa happily said.

" Abhi jagi hoti toh bohot sawaal karti aapko dekh ke..." Karishma said.

" Aap madam sir se milli..." Karishma asked.

" Nhi usse rehne dein uski Ammi ke paas...kal aaram se mil lungi...." Maa said smiling.

" Ab Anu ke paas jati hu...usse bohot saari baate karni hai..." Maa said
kissing Karishma's forehead.

" Shaadi ki bhi baat karna..." Karishma said.

" Badmaash...ye bhi koi batane ki baat hai..." Maa chuckled.

The peaceful night bought peace in the lives.

The adorable mothers are back!!!

Keep reading" THE AFTERMATH "

Do vote & comment.

"Remember votes & comments, motivate me to write the next part early "

" Votes & Comments are key to early & interesting updates "

~ Kishaaa

Hitched

A special recommendation Switch your page to dark mode to enjoy and feel this part !!!

" Humne kaha na....nhi rahoge tum dono sath mein.." Ammi strictly warned.

" Lekin Ammi...." A sad Haseena whinned.

" Pehle hum nhi the yaha...toh rehliya na saat mein....ab jabtak shaadi nhi hojati tab alag...." Maa ordered.

" Aap kuch kahiye na...." Haseena murmured against Anubhav but Anubhav couldn't speak anything to which Haseena gave a angry glare.

" Chal Haseena tera samaan humare room mein le chal..." Ammi ordered.

" Mai aarahi tere saath rahungi..." Maa ordered Anubhav.

" Shaadi ke baad toh ek hi room mein rahoge na...toh abhi 4 dino se kya jaa raha...chal mera baccha chal mere saath..." Ammi buttered Haseena.

Haseena sadly stormed of to her room leaving Anubhav scared.Now he had to face his dearest priye moreover her bestfriend her taunts which never left her may it be any situation.

" Priye bas 3 din ki hi toh baat hai..." Anubhav said to Haseena who just putting all the clothes in her bag.

" Priye....aap aise kyu kar rhi...." Anubhav said.

" Aapko bolna bhi aata hai...par bahar toh aap kuch bole hi nhi..." Haseena said with an extra sweet smile which of course scared Anubhav.

" Bas tin din reh lijiye phir hum dono ek saath rahenge...." Anubhav back hugged her.

" Chodiye Anubhav humara mood nhi hai...." Haseena came out of the hug and left with her bag.

" Prabhu ab aap hi dijiye inhe manane ki takad..." Anubhav seeked strength to apologize his grumpy to be wife.

" Mamu chalo na bahar...hume khelna hai aapke saath..." Little Mithii said holding Anubhav's wrist.

" Abhi bohot raat hogayi hai Mithii....hum subah khelenge...." Anubhav said.

" Itni bhi raat nhi hui hai...bas 9 hi toh baj rahe hai...chalo mami bhi khelne wali hai mere saath..." Mithii knew what to say!

Anubhav went out to the hall with Mithii where he saw Haseena with a grumpy face but he was helpless.

"Baitho...Dadi....Nani..Amminani..Amma...aao na..." Mithii said distributing the cards in different sets with Mihir's help.

" Shivani tujhe kya alag se batao aana jaldi..." Mithii scolded Shivani.

" Aarahi hu meri maa...." Shivani said settling beside Amar.

" Tu maa nhi hai meri.ye meri Amma hai..." Mithii said giggling pointing at Karishma which made everyone smile even the grumpy Haseena.

" Chalo...Lambe pol shuru karo..." Mithii ordered Amar.

" Jara toh sharam karo...Tumhara jija banne wala hu...lanbe pole kya laga rakha hai..." Amar said .

" Amar sir...agar aap Mithii ke jija ban gaye....toh aapki height kam nhi hojayegi...tabhi bhi aap lambe pol hi rahenge...." Santosh said the truth.

" Santuji control rakhiye apni maasumiyat par..." Cheetah murmured against her.

" Pehle sirf Karishma madam kisi bolti band karwa sakti thi....ab dekho ye mitha bomb bhi unhi ki rah par chal raha hai..." Billu said.

" Aare billu aakhir humari bahu aur poti hai..." Pushpaji proudly said making everyone widen their eyes.

" Aap please khelo na....badbad mat karo..." Mithii irritatedly said._____
____

Returning

Author's POV

All the bags packed were kept in the hall of Pawar Vada.While others were getting ready for their departure.Yess it was the day when our dearly people were returning to Lucknow.Mahila Police Thana was now renovated and was ready to secure the city of Lucknow.It was nearly 10 months since the heart wrenching incident.Today all the patriots were happily returning to their home to their town LUCKNOW!!____________

" Madam sir please meri baat samajhne ki koshish kijiyr...." Santosh pleaded to Haseena who standing there with a stern expression on her face folding her hands.

" Hum joh keh diya...woh keh diya..." Haseena said with the same expression.

" Madam sir...mai nhi jana chahtii cyber cell wapas..." Santosh sadly said.

" Mujhe aap sabke saath milke kaam karna hai..." Santosh stated.

" Hume samaj nhi aaraha aap samaj kyu nhi rhi hai...ye aapke career ke lite bohot important point hai...peak point hai ye aapka " Haseena tried to explain.

" Madam sir...please samjhne ki koshish kijiye mai nhi reh sakti aap sabke bina....mai pehle ye sab experience kar chuki hu...Aur mai waha bilkul khush nhi thi..." Santosh almost spoke crying.

" Aur aap hi kehti haina...jaha par aap khush nhi hai...waha par aapko nhi rehna chahiye...toh phir aap mujhe jane ke liye kyu keh rhi hai..." A broken Santosh asked Haseena.

" Pichli baar aise hi aapne mujhe emotional karke...mithi mithi baate sunakar bhej diya cyber cell....par iss bar nhi jaungi mein kisi ki nhi sun ugi..." Santosh declared.

" Aap nhi janti madam sir...Mai aap logo ko kya manti hu...Aap sab duniya hai meri..." Santosh said and Haseena looked at her emotionally.

" Bohot mushkil hai mere liye akele rehna...na waha ke log acche hai na sen ior...please madam sir mat kijiye mujhe aap sabse dur..." Santosh requested and Haseena somewhat understood her condition.

" Maami...chalo jaldi...train aajayegii..." Mithii knocked at the door.

" Aap jaiye bahar...hum aate hai...." Haseena said in cold voice.

" Lekin...." Santosh was about to say but was cut off.

" Hume abhi nikalna hai...baad mein baat karenge..." Haseena said turning herself in other direction.

Wiping her tears and glancing at Haseena,Santosh left the room.Outside everyone glanced at Santosh and had an idea about what happened insid e.________

A

uthor's POV

The sweet people reached the railway junction vistimg the famous Ganesha TempleMithii's Bappa!!They were free today.Their faces shining bright.

Amar and Shivani were returning back to Mumbai they had already sent Shivani's parents next day of the marriage and same with Haseena and Anubhav.______________

" Sach kahu toh bohot man horaha hai...tun sabke saath jane ka...Par abhi duty bhi join karni jaruri hai....bohot din hogaye hai.." Shivani expressed.

" Ha...mujhe bhi thana dekhna tha...par koi nai hum dono jaldi Lucknow aayenge..." Amar said.

" Jarur aaiye...." Anubhav said.

" Aur Shivani....phirse thank you hum sab ki jaan bachane ke liye..." Haseena thanked her.

" Kya re...jazbaat wali bai...tum abhi mujhe dost nhi mani...mat bolna thank you...dost haina tu meri..." Shivani said hugging her.

" Shivani...thank you...tumne hume sabse bada tofa diya hai...Agar hum aaj yaha nhi hote toh...Mithii humari nhi hoti..." Karishma thanked.

" Dekh...jo jiske naseeb main hota hai...wo usse mil jata hai...koi usse chin nhi sakta..." Shivani stated the fact.

" Toh phir jaldi milenge..." Mihir said shaking hands with Amar.

" Tu mumbai ja rahi hai..." Mithii asked Shivani.

" Ha toh mera ghar toh wahi hai..." Shivani said.

" Matlab tum mere saath nhi aaogi..." Mithii asked

" Aaungi na...mai tujse na milu aisa hosakta hai kya..." Shivani said taking Mithii into her arms.

" Mat jao na mumbai...mere saath chalo..." Mithii emotionally said.

" Aisa nhi hota Mithii...Mera ghar kaam sab wahi hai...mujhe jana hoga..." Shivani said careesing her cheek.

" Par mujhe tumhari yaad aayegi..." Mithii said teary.

" Aree toh yaad aayegi toh phone karle...phone hai na tere amma papa ke paas...." Shivani tried to explain.

" Par phone pein mai tujhe gale toh nhi laga paungii na..." Mithii said hugging Shivani crying.

" Tu ro kyu rhi hai Mithii...mai jaldi tujse milne aaungi..." Shivani said wiping her tears.

" Pakka...." Mithii asked.

" Ha pakka...Aai shapath..." Shivani promised.

Shifting a sad Mithi to Karishma's arms Shivani and Amar boarded their train and waved a goodbye to MPT family.

" Chaliye humari bhi train aagayii hai..." Cheetah said and everyone walked towards the entrance.

www.ingramcontent.com/pod-product-compliance
Lightning Source LLC
Chambersburg PA
CBHW070344200726
48294CB00003B/787